To Sue, Mary & Laura

I hope you enjoy this book. Best Wishes

[signature]

September 2014

deadly violin

A MYSTERY NOVEL

ROBERT MITCHELL

LOUDOUN HOUSE BOOKS
2013

ISBN—978-62407-821-7

To Jean,
For her encouragement, tolerance,
suggestions...and most of all listening.

~ACKNOWLEDGEMENTS~

Miguel Linares for historical research assistance; Bill Gardner, my sons Scott and Todd Mitchell and Adventure Creative Group for support and advise; Marv Holt for first read; and Sandy Holt for first read and her invaluable editorial help .

deadly violin

Prologue

Giuseppe Guarneri, who later became known as Joseph de Gesú (because of how he sometimes labeled his violins), is known as one of the most illustrious violin-makers in history. Today many of his violins are regarded as equal to those of Stradivarius—some even superior.

He came from a long line of master craftsmen who for over a hundred years were a family of violin-makers working and living in Cremona, Italy. This small provincial town was well known for its luthiers—the Amati family, Antonio Stradivarius, Carlo Bergonzi and Guarneri.

Stradivarius, his competitor across the piazza, was still consistently producing violins at the age of eighty-six. Upon his death at ninety-three, Stradivarius was said to have eighty-two violins in his shop. But Guarneri was neither prolific nor consistent. He rarely had more than a few.

Like the rest of Europe at the time, Italy was swept up in a passion for music, and Italian music was inseparably connected to its violin-makers. But unlike the more sedate music of England and France, Italian music was constructed for the passion and outrageous expression of the theatre. John Dryden noted this change in music for the violin:

> **Sharp violins proclaim**
> **Their jealous pangs, and desperation,**
> **Fury, frantic indignation,**
> **Depths of pains, and heights of passion,**
> **For the fair, disdainful dame.**

This is a tale of the most carefully constructed violin that Giuseppe Guarneri made—and it would be his last. It was conceived in love and cut and shaped with passion. He intended it to be special and unique. Indeed it was. In this story, upon the violin were played the last sounds he would ever hear. As if cursed, this violin would continue to be surrounded by murder, mystery and intrigue. Disappearing and out-of-sight for well over two hundred years, this legendary violin finally emerged only a few hundred miles from where it was crafted. Its reputation survived, for its sonorous tones belie the tragedy and sorrow that befall those who take it in their grasp. It is a somber tune it plays for those who seek its allure or hope to possess this priceless treasure.

Part One

Chapter One

Paint brush in hand, Giuseppe Guarneri looked up from his workbench as two strangers entered his shop at n° 7 Piazza S. Prospero. It is 1774, and unseasonably cold for October in Cremona, Italy. The collars of the men's cloaks are pulled up to their ears and a cold draft entered the violin shop with them..

"Buon giorno, Signore," said the taller of the men, stepping forward.

"How can I help you?" asked Giuseppe, setting his brush back in the varnish pot.

"We are traders from Venice," he said, referring to his companion. "Since we are in Cremona we hoped we might procure several violins...that is, if we could get a good price."

Giuseppe Guarneri hesitated as he studied the men. He felt a curious uneasiness. The cut of their clothes and their shapeless shoes did not suggest successful middle class merchants. The tall man seemed pleasant enough, although perhaps a bit uncomfortable. To Giuseppe the man was transparent. He was what he seemed to be...an artful schemer, with an engaging manner and a glib tongue.

It was the other man, the short little man who had not spoken. He had hard eyes, which occasionally darted furtively about the room. His aquiline nose conformed to his chiseled face. But it was his dark complexion. It seemed out of place in Lombardy and the other regions of northern Italy. Maybe Sardinian...or perhaps Corsican, Giuseppe thought. The man had a scar beginning at the corner of his mouth and extending to his chin, giving him a kind of perpetual sneer—a little smile of contempt.

Suddenly there was a noise above the shop and the sound of someone coming down the stairs. It was Catterina, the violin maker's wife. She had heard voices and came down to investigate. She stood at the bottom of the staircase, looking inquisitively at the strangers.

The tall man quickly took off his hat, unclasped his cloak and threw it over his arm. The short dark man took his cue and did the same, for they were in the presence of the lady of the house.

Even in her house dress and cap, Catterina Roda Guarneri is strikingly attractive. At forty-three years old she has lost but little of her youthful figure. Her dress dips precipitously at the neck, for this is the beginning of the Age of Enlightenment, and despite the Church's protestations it is the fashion of the day. In mediation perhaps, a little silver cross hangs from a red silk ribbon around her neck. Catterina was born in the Tyrol, and her Austrian origins are evident from errant wisps of blond hair escaping from under her cap. Her facial features and fair complexion are more Nordic than Southern European. It is apparent that she is a forceful presence in the house as she stands, arms folded across her chest, scrutinizing the strange men.

"Signori, this is my wife Catterina Guarneri." Giuseppe joined his wife, who had not moved from the bottom of the stair case. "These men are traders from Venice and are looking to buy violins while here in Cremona." He turned and addressed the men directly. "Unfortunately I seldom carry an inventory of violins for sale. Customers place an order and I can usually complete the work within three weeks"...Giuseppe quickly glanced at his wife..."sometimes more. The violins hanging here are orders waiting to be picked up. The one that I was working on when you came in...well, that is a special circumstance. It is not for sale, and in any case is not finished. Had I known you were coming—"

"What, exactly," asked Catterina, "might you be willing to pay?"

The tall man hesitated. "Four or five lire?"

"Ah," said Giuseppe "I'm afraid that would not have been possible. Not for my violins."

The tall man draped his cloak over his shoulders. Obviously there was no business to be done here.

Catterina advanced toward the men. "Tell me, you say you are from Venice...then as traders you must know of my husband's brother—Nicolo Guarneri. He is well known as a violin maker there."

"Nicolo?" The man's eyes widened. "Why yes...well I don't know him personally, but I understand that he does very nice work."

Giuseppe looked inquisitively at his wife.

Catterina continued: "What other merchandise do you deal in?"

"Jewelry, silver plate...most anything of value," said the tall man, as both men fastened their cloaks and began pulling up their collars. They appeared ill at ease and anxious to leave.

"Arrividerci," said Giuseppe with an indifferent little wave.

The men bowed to Catterina and, after a nod to her husband, in a swirl of cool October air they closed the door behind them.

They stood for a moment. Giuseppe chuckled and shook his head.

A broad smile widened Catterina's face. "I think we know what they are not," she said. "They are not traders and they are not from Venice. They were lying."

"You lied to *them*!"

"Not really. Your brother does make violins in Venice. Of course he is Pietro Guarneri...not Nicolo. I just baited the trap. He caught himself." She paused, "I didn't like them. They smelled of pipe smoke and garlic, and that's a bad combination."

"The smaller man smelled like trouble, if you ask me," replied Giuseppe.

Catterina turned and started up the stairs. "I'm going up and make some supper."

"Good. That will give me time to finish here. This violin needs to start drying," said Giuseppe, reaching for the varnish pot.

Half way up the stairs, Catterina turned. "What troubles me, is who really are they...and what did they want here? The other man—the one who never spoke, he frightens me. He was as cold as ice. I felt a chill in his presence."

"*Cara mia*, "don't worry. Whatever they wanted, could it be found here?" Giuseppe returned to his work. "Let me finish here. You always wanted a violin...your own violin. I want you to have it for your birthday and I have only three days before the seventeenth."

"*Amore mio*, would that you were always so industrious. Oh, I do want to play it for you. And I'm very curious to hear how it sounds." Catterina disappeared up the stairs.

Giuseppe took up his brush. There was *something* about the strangers in his shop. He thought he had seen a glint in the folds of the little man's waist band...where one would carry a knife. Could it be? If so, it was small. Perhaps a dirk. Or, possibly he had just imagined it. The violin maker caressed the violin with light, even strokes of his brush. The oil varnish was soft in quality and light in texture...a rich lustrous orange-brown, with perhaps the slightest tinge of red. He was known in the trade for the superb quality of his wood and varnish. If it was sunny tomorrow he would hang it in the window. This violin must dry naturally, but it must be finished by October seventeenth...Catterina's forty-first birthday.

As the familiar smell of varnish filled the little shop, Giuseppe's mind wandered. Making this violin for Catterina was giving him great pleasure. It was a good feeling to do something he could be proud of. He had not been a good husband, and he knew it.

Giuseppe had always been of independent character. His father had been a prominent violin maker in Cremona, but Giuseppe had left home to make his own way in life. He met Catterina, who was captivated by his handsome features and bold, sometimes brash manner. They married, and after living a number of years with her family in the Tyrol, returned to settle in Cremona, where Giuseppe set up shop as a violin maker. He did so, not because of a passion for his craft, but simply because he needed a source of income. Unless asked, he never bothered to sign or label his work. His extraordinary talent as a luither nevertheless produced violins of superb tonal quality.

His problem was that in Cremona the violin trade had long been dominated by a flamboyant craftsman just across the Piazza. Antonio Stradivari, at the advanced age of eighty-six still passionately sold violins to the Church, nobility or musicians of the Ducal Courts. For his violins he received two or three times more than Giuseppe could ever obtain.

As a result, Giuseppe made his violins for fiddlers who entertained the populace and received little reward for their effort. To meet the competition, he was forced to work fast and loose. Haste became his execution.

Training in his father's shop taught him the technical and manual skills necessary to produce high quality instruments, which he invariably did. He never resorted to using cheaper woods—unlike his violin-making family and even Stradivari himself. However, Giuseppe's measurements for each violin were never the same. His sides not quite accurately bent. Sound holes were placed on the whim of the moment. Gouge and chisel work was sometimes deft, sometimes crude.

Nevertheless, Giuseppe's work showed a freedom from restraint—a departure from tradition that made his violins distinctive. It would have been much simpler to merely reproduce that which had gone before. But like the man himself, each of his violins displayed their independence…with unique tonal quality unlike any other.

Some who knew Giuseppe Guarneri considered him lazy, unreliable and irresponsible. He had long been a heavy drinker, and despite a few feeble attempts to quit the bottle, he could not resist his wine, brandy, ale and occasionally when available, the new gin. For many years, Catterina would wait up for him to return from the neighborhood taverns. Now, she would simply lock the door—leaving it unbarred from the inside, and put a candle lamp in the upstairs window to help guide him home. Besides drink, there were rumors of Giuseppe's involvement in "other pleasures of the world".

It was not a happy marriage. Living with Giuseppe was hard. Nevertheless, Catterina maintained a deep love for her husband. She often helped him make his violins, and watched over him as best she could. Maybe children would have moderated his behavior…perhaps not. In any event, they could not have a child. They never had an apprentice in the shop nor a maid or servant in the house. It was often a lonely place.

As Giuseppe turned to his drink, Catterina would pick up a violin in the shop and turn to her music. When she was a young girl her parents sent her to a music conservatory in Salzburg, which inspired her interest in music and talent as a violinist. There was no opera or public concerts in Cremona. She, however, was a member of an informal group of local musicians who managed to organize a few occasional performances. Music filled an obvious void in her life. Now she was to have her own violin. She was almost giddy at the thought of it.

Chapter Two

The next day was clear and sunny. Catterina stood in the little shop window at n°7 on the piazza. The last sunlight of the day filtered through the window and fell on the violin hanging there. She admired the detail and care with which her husband had crafted her violin.

Although generally well constructed, in the last two or three years his violins were made without precision or detail. Lack of care in his work and the steadiness of his hands were becoming casualties of his lifestyle.

But this violin was different from the rest. It was a bit smaller than the traditional fourteen inches…more feminine. He had thrown all his energy and mastery of the art into her birthday gift. The detail of the design, the even finish of the edge, accurate inlay of the purfling and the careful placement and cutting of the ʃ-holes, were an amazing affirmation of his skill.

It had not come easily. He used one trembling hand to steady the other. His forehead glistened with perspiration as he guided the chisel, gauge and file to do that which once was accomplished by a single stroke. Many times he set the work aside in anguish and frustration.

Catterina had not heard him enter behind her.

"Do you like it?" he asked quietly.

She turned. "It's lovely." She wrapped her arms around him. They held each other tightly, standing there in a silent, unspoken expression of what might have been.

They parted. 'Will you be home tonight?" She knew the probable answer.

Once the sun was setting, darkness came fast to Cremona. The three and four story buildings that crowded the narrow streets quickly shut out any remaining daylight. Children were called in from play. Shopkeepers shuttered their windows. The lamplighter, his little ladder over his shoulder, was starting to make his rounds. Women began reeling in their clothes that had been hanging to dry over the streets and alleys. Below, on the cobblestones, Giuseppe made his way, as he had countless times before, to his favorite taverns.

Cane in hand he moved along at a jaunty pace. Canes were no longer reserved for the nobility. Many men now carried them, especially after dark. They were useful defensive weapons against dogs, street ruffians and other nefarious rouges and scoundrels. The canes generally had heavy heads of porcelain, silver, ivory or wood, and were often weighted with a bit of lead. Giuseppe's silver-headed cane had a hidden feature. The lower end was hollow and could be pulled off to expose the long thin shaft of a stiletto set into the top half of the cane. He had never needed to use this little rapier-like sword, but it made him feel more secure when out on his nightly trysts with the bottle.

Tonight he had the vague feeling that he was being watched. He probably was. Commerce had ceased for the day and there were but few good reasons to be out after dark. The occasional passers-by cautiously eyed each other with suspicion, and scanned the shadows for anyone that might be lurking there.

Giuseppe paused to cross the street as a carriage-for-hire clattered by. The driver tipped his hat in acknowledgment, and in a few more steps the violin maker reached the door to the *Vescovi Dito.* The "Bishop's Finger" was a tavern in which he was a familiar figure. The tavern's name was meant to imply a saintly bishop pointing the way to righteousness, although most of its patrons generally had another interpretation. Giuseppe stepped inside and surveyed the room. His gaze fell on a lone man sitting at a table. He was facing the door, and Giuseppe immediately recognized him as the tall stranger in his shop.

For a moment he considered leaving, but curiosity prevailed. The man had been watching the door, and rose in greeting.

"Ah, the violin master," he said, offering his hand. "Would you care to join me? I'd be privileged if you'd let me buy you a glass of ale."

Giuseppe seldom drank ale. By the time it was brought down from the northern countries it was often stale...but he would not reject the offer of a drink.

"I thought you had probably gone back to...ah, Venice."

The man signaled the bar maid for another ale. "Not yet. Not for two days. I'm about done here, but my business partner has a few more things to take care of. He couldn't join me tonight...he is not feeling well. The grippe, I think. By the way, my name is Benito—Benito Rastelli."

"Are you staying here? In the rooms upstairs?"

Benito put down his glass, wiping his moustache with the back of his hand. "No, a few blocks up the street."

"Do you have a wife? Children?"

"Yes, two children, but I don't see them much. Being on the road, you know."

They continued talking and drinking into the night. Every time someone entered the tavern, Benito looked up. Pork sausages were ordered. More ale followed. This man, Giuseppe thought, was generous, if not particularly good company.

The night wore on. Now only a few other patrons remained. Giuseppe thought he heard the door open. Benito looked up with a nearly imperceptible glimmer of recognition...but when Giuseppe turned there was no one there. Benito lifted his glass and after wiping his moustache one last time, he took out a pocket watch.

"I didn't realize it was so late. I must be going." He stood and they said their goodbyes.

Giuseppe stayed a few minutes to finish his glass, then walked into the cool air of the street. There was no one in sight. He walked more slowly now, a bit unsteady, with his cane feeling the way over the cobblestones.

Alone, above the violin shop, Catterina read by candlelight until her eyes grew weary. Then, after placing the customary candle lamp in the window, climbed into bed and soon fell asleep. Once, she thought she heard her husband coming home. She listened for a moment...then fell back asleep. He would be home eventually. He always did.

It was later than usual when she heard him fumbling with his key in the lock. Giuseppe entered, barred the door from the inside, and began feeling his way up the stairs. Catterina stirred as he entered the room. Soon the light was blown out. Silence and darkness fell over the Guarneri house.

The next morning, the fifteenth of October, Catterina was stirring breakfast porridge when there was a shout from the workshop downstairs. She hurried down to find Giuseppe staring at the wall.

"They're gone!" he yelled, gesturing wildly. "All four violins are gone. The one I'm making for you wasn't finished, so they didn't take it, but the others are all gone!"

"Nothing like this has ever happened," said Catterina—a chilling realization setting in. "It had to be the strangers. It's just too much of a coincidence."

Giuseppe paced angrily around the shop. "Must have come in after I left—and before I came home and barred the door."

Catterina was feeling very vulnerable. "These locks are easily opened for anyone who knows how. I was alone upstairs..." her voice dropped off.

"It was the little man," said Giuseppe, "the one with the hard eyes...the one who never spoke. I ran into his companion at the tavern. He bought me drinks and supper. It must have been to keep me occupied—to keep me away from home." He felt an overwhelming and all too familiar mixture of guilt and shame. After breakfast he would go out and report the theft. Not that he thought it would do much good.

The local police were an informal group of loosely organized volunteers and appointed townspeople charged with upholding the law. For the most part, they occupied themselves with discouraging minor street crime. They had little time and few resources for crime investigation or for what was considered simply common misbehavior. Matters of greater importance or civil disobedience were handled by the local garrison of the Imperial Austrian army, who had maintained a presence in Cremona for decades.

At the local police station, Giuseppe learned that the watchmaker across the piazza had also been robbed during the night. Two men had reportedly been in the shop earlier in the day. They matched the description of the strangers in the violin shop. The lone police officer on duty offered his condolences over Giuseppe's misfortune and, with a shrug, promised the constabulary would respond to any reports of men matching this description.

Despite Catterina's protestations, Giuseppe could not bring himself to let it go. His vindictive nature would not permit it. He could not rely on the police. He would try to find these men himself.

Chapter Three

It was early evening, but it was already dark and a light rain was falling. The dim glow of candles and lamps filled windows along the shadowy streets. In the cold mist, the violin maker made his way toward the *Bishop's Finger*. Here and there the tops of cobblestones glistened in an occasional shaft of light. The wet air was heavy with the smell of horses and centuries of human habitation. The tavern would be his first stop in the search for the two thieves. He had no idea where it might lead. He also knew that it was possible the men had already left the city.

The familiar and welcome smells of the tavern greeted him as he pushed open the door. Customers, hunched over their drinks, looked up as he entered. The man he was looking for was standing behind the bar drying glasses. Agustino was the proprietor, and in a position to hear…and overhear, the undertones of the darker life of the city. Moreover, he was known to enjoy gossip and rumor, and if any one might know anything about the two strangers it would be Agustino.

The tavern owner stepped from behind the bar as he saw Giuseppe approaching. His apron did little to contain his rotund shape, which stretched tightly around his considerable girth. Deeply set into his apple-cheeked face were mischievous eyes which betrayed a knowledge of things only to be spoken of in hushed tones.

"Benevento, Giuseppe," he said, extending a pudgy hand. "Can I get you something to drink?"

"Perhaps another time. Augustino, I need some information."

Augustino's face grew into a sly smile. He drew closer to invite the query.

"Do you remember the man I was with last night?"

The proprietor nodded.

"I need to know if you know anything about him…or a small man that he is often seen with."

"Ah…does this have something to do with the robbery of your shop last night?"

"Perhaps—"

"No. Actually I thought you knew him. The small man was never in here. I saw him at the door several times…looking in, but he never came in."

"I thought he might be staying in one of your rooms upstairs?"

"Giuseppe, you know I don't have rooms for overnight. The rooms are for the girls here—and their friends." "But," he pulled at his moustache thoughtfully, "You should talk to Carlota. She is our most popular bar maid, and knows most of the other *prostitutas* in Cremona. She hears things I don't"

Augustino motioned across the room, summoning a young woman to the bar. The woman, taking her cue, crossed provocatively to the two men.

"Carlota, this is Signore Guarneri. He would like to talk to you. I would like you to help him if you can."

Carlota stood there, demurely twirling strands of hair around her fingers. She looked to be in her mid-twenties, and if not beautiful, certainly attractive with a freshness and innocence that belied her life as a *prostituta*. With a coquettish cock of the head she asked, "What can I do for you?"

"Carlota, I need information. Things that you may have heard on the street."

Suddenly her expression and demeanor changed. "All right. What?"

"I was in here last night with a man, drinking and eating. In fact, you served us early in the evening. Do you know anything about this man…where he might be staying in Cremona?"

"I remember him. I didn't see either of you leave. I got…busy. I never saw him before last night and I don't know anything about him. I'm sorry."

In desperation, Giuseppe asked "There was another man—who was often seen with him. He was a little man, dark complexion, hard looking. He had a scar on his face."

Carlota's eyes grew wide. Then narrowed. A flicker of anger crossed her face. "The scar—it was at the corner of his mouth. It made him look mean."

"Yes! That's the man. You know him?"

"I know *about* him," she hissed. "He beat up one of the girls who works on the north side. Nice girl too. At a place called"…she smiled, *"Il Gallo Felice."*

He had to think fast. He would either have to try to catch the thief by surprise at "The Happy Rooster"—or, somehow entice the man to meet with him.

Giuseppe gently took Carlota's arm. "Do you think you could arrange for him to meet me?"

"I don't see how."

"Here's how. It may work." He led Carlotta to a secluded table in the corner, and with their heads nearly touching in hushed tones he laid out his plan.

Several minutes passed before they drew apart, and Giuseppe pressed a silver necklace into her hand. It was set with small rubies and diamonds. It was one of Catterina's most treasured family possessions.

Carlotta slipped it into her pocket and after a few words to Augustino, threw on her cape and with Giuseppe quietly left the tavern. It was still early evening. The weather was foul and few people were out. The two hooded figures hurried through the mist toward the *Il Gallo Felice.*

As luck would have it, the little thief was at the tavern without his partner. The two conspirators knew they should no longer be seen together. They were anxious to leave Cremona, but had not been able to book the road carriage to Verona until the 19th of October. It would be necessary for them to remain as inconspicuous as possible for two more days.

According to plan, Giuseppe waited in a doorway a few buildings away, while Carlotta entered the tavern to find—or learn, the whereabouts of the little man.

Inside the dimly lit tavern the air was heavy with pipe smoke and the smell of stale ale. Carlotta attracted the attention of a few men who looked up with more than idle curiosity. She scanned the room for the man with the crooked smile but he was nowhere to be seen. Finally she caught the eye of one of the working girls, who paused with a tray of glasses as Carlotta approached.

"*Whatever* are you doing here?" the wide-eyed girl whispered.

Carlotta took her by the arm and drew her close. "We've known each other for a long time. Since we were school girls. I need a favor. I am looking for a man…a small man, with a scar running down his chin."

The young woman's eyes grew thin and hard. "The one who hurt a friend of mine…a girl who works here. Yes, I know him."

"Did she report it?"

"It was in his room upstairs. Offered her half a lire to see him. We never can ask that much here, so she went. After she gave him what he wanted he started choking her—and took his money back."

"But she didn't tell anyone?"

"No. I saw her stumble back down the stairs. She was crying. She told me all about it, but of course she couldn't tell the owner and risk losing her job here. At best, he would have told her she should have been more careful. It's the way it is here".

"This man—do you know where he is now?"

The girl smiled grimly and nodded toward a dark corner of the tavern. "The *sadico* is sitting right there!"

Carlotta squinted, and through the gloomy haze saw a small figure at a table in the far corner. Drawing a deep breath, she struggled to maintain an air of confidence as she strolled toward the man.

"Well, what do we have here?" he said with a feeble attempt at courtesy.

Without waiting to be invited she boldly sat and looked him directly in the eyes. She wrestled to repress the alarm and revulsion she felt. It was if she was looking into the face of the devil himself.

Without flinching, she said "Look—I know who you are and I don't much care. I have business to conduct, and if you are not interested I will be on my way."

His eyes narrowed suspiciously. "What business would that be?"

For an instant she was stunned by his voice. It was thin and raspy—almost a hiss. She sensed that this was a very dangerous man, and no one to be trifled with. "My boyfriend has a habit of coming into possession of things of considerable value. I sell them for him." She reached into her pocket. "I thought you might—"

The man cut her short. "I don't know what made you think that I would be interested is such a thing. Take it elsewhere. Leave me alone."

"Very well," said Carlotta, feigning indifference and dangling the necklace before his eyes. Even in the dim light the gem encrusted necklace caught sharp glints of diamonds encircling rubies, along with the gleam of a brilliant emerald suspended from the silver chain. "I thought perhaps a perceptive man like you might see the extraordinary value of something like this."

Without warning, he grabbed her by the wrist, but with her other hand Carlotta snatched away the necklace, returning it to her pocket.

The man glanced about the room. Suddenly his demeanor changed. He let go of her arm and attempting a conciliatory tone, he hissed "If I *was* interested, how much?"

"I'm told it's worth at least thirty Imperial lire. But, on the—shall we say secondary market…ten lire."

"Five lire" said the man with a crooked smile.

"Seven'" countered Carlotta. She knew he would not hesitate to rob her by force if he had the chance, for it would be a theft that could not be reported.

"He did not hesitate. "*Bene*, but I don't have that much in my pocket. I have a room upstairs. We will go there, and I will pay you."

Carlotta smiled wickedly. "No" she said firmly, "I *know* how you treat women in your room. I'll meet you outside…three doors away, under the street lamp. If you are not there in ten minutes I will be gone."

He paused, considering the logistics, then rose from the table. "In a few minutes."

Carlotta pulled up the hood of her cloak for protection from the cold mist and fog, and hurried to join Giuseppe hiding in the shadows of a nearby doorway. After a few words she handed him the necklace, and in return he pressed some coins into her palm.

Anxious minutes passed before a small figure left the tavern. For a full minute he stood motionless, surveying the street. It was deserted except for the hooded silhouette waiting for him under the dim glow of the street lamp. Satisfied that he could overpower her without being seen, he approached her. He reached out to grab his quarry when suddenly it turned.

Giuseppe seized him by the shoulders, shoving him violently back against a stone building. Taken by surprise, the man put up little resistance. Then he sprang alive. Giuseppe felt the man's sinewy muscles straining, as he fought back. It was like trying to restrain a wildcat. He jammed his forearm against the man's throat. "Where are my violins?"

The man did not answer and continued to struggle.

"The violins you stole! Tell me!" It was all Giuseppe could do to maintain control. "Tell me! Or I swear I'll—" He felt a sudden movement of the man, then a sharp, searing pain in his stomach. For a briefest moment he thought he had been hit in the abdomen. Then he felt the dagger being withdrawn. As Giuseppe fell to his knees the thief broke free and with a swirl of his cloak the little man quickly disappeared into the darkness. It had all happened so fast.

The violin maker began tottering home, his arms wrapped around himself. Perhaps it was the rush of excitement, for the pain was somewhat tolerable. He slipped his hand inside his waistband as he walked. It was wet and sticky but didn't seem to be bleeding badly. If he could just make it home…

It was only six or seven blocks. The few people he encountered assumed he was a drunk stumbling by, and if anybody recognized him it merely confirmed their suspicions. He was taking little steps now. It didn't hurt so much that way. Nevertheless each one now provoked an agonizing stab of pain deep in his stomach. Tiny beads of clammy perspiration erupted on his forehead from the exertion. Each block seemed longer than the last, and the evening air cold and inhospitable. He felt chilled and occasional waves of shivering shook his body. His only thought now was to make it home. To Catterina.

Mercifully he finally reached the doorstep to *n° 7* in *Piazza S. Prospero.* She heard him fumbling with the lock. It was still relatively early in the evening and Catterina was still awake. He seemed to be taking an unusually long time with the lock and she started down the stairs with the lantern to greet him.

She was nearly at the bottom step when the door swung slowly open to reveal Giuseppe teetering in the doorway. Instantly she knew something was terribly wrong. Catterina helped him upstairs, a slow agonizing climb, as he related his fight with the little thief. She helped him undress, and discovered her necklace in his pocket. Both embarrassed and apologetic, Giuseppe explained how he had used it to lure the man into the street.

She put him to bed, where she examined the puncture wound. In the glow of the lantern a slight trickle of blood oozed from the slit in his stomach. It was obvious that any serious damage would be internal. She covered him with thick blankets, and to ease the pain gave him three drops of tincture of opium. Eventually he drifted off into a fitful sleep.

Early the next morning, October 16th, Catterina sent for the doctor. He was a kindly old man who had seen much sickness and sorrow. Examining the wound he clucked between clenched teeth, but said nothing.

Finally he drew Catterina aside. "I am not hopeful," he said, "but miracles do happen. He is a strong man and still relatively young, but the wound is deep. Much deeper than I want to probe. There is really nothing more I can do. As you see, he has a high temperature. That is not a good sign. If it becomes more than day fever, then—"

"Doctor, what can I do for him?"

"Make him as comfortable as possible. Occasionally apply cool cloths on his forehead. Give him as much water as he will take. If the corruption in the abdomen becomes black fever, likely the shakes will follow. You will soon know."

"And if…it does turn bad," she asked plaintively?

He put his arm around her. Dear *signori,* all you can do is continue the opiate…four or five drops every four hours. Sooner if the pain becomes severe. When—if he becomes restless and starts to talk about imaginary things you may want to give him a full spoon of the tincture of opium. Do you have enough?"

Catterina nodded.

"Very well, then. However much you give him at that point, it will not only ease his suffering, but shorten his agony—and God will not fault you."

After a few more kind words he left. Catterina was left alone with her husband of twenty years.

The day wore on. It became apparent that he was not getting better. Giuseppe himself knew it. They talked of their early years together…of more carefree times. And when the pain killer wore off he tossed in agony and begged for more.

The sun began to set and cast shadows across the street. Catterina left her husband and went to the kitchen for a few scraps of bread and cheese. When she returned he reached out for her. She took his hand in hers.

"*Amore*," he said softly, "there is something I must say—something you must hear." Tears swelled in the rim of his eyes. "I have not loved you the way you deserved to be loved. But I *have* loved you. I always have. Perhaps I have simply been the best husband I could be—but not the one I should have been and wanted to be. I'm sorry..."

He tightened his eyes as a spasm of pain swept his body, forcing the tears to his cheeks. Catterina smiled and placed her finger to his lips, but he had more to say…

"You are a good woman, Catterina. You deserved better than me. I am nothing but a selfish fool. Thank you for staying with me all these years."

She again placed her finger tips on his lips to silence him, and lay down beside his feverish body and held him in her arms. "Shush. Giuseppe, we *are* who we *are*. Don't you know in my own way I was happy with you? I choose you. You are *my* man."

They lay there for a while. Then he spoke. "I have one more thing to ask of you," he said weakly. "Will you play for me? On you own violin. I set the bridge and strung it yesterday. It needs to be played—to be heard."

He could hear her tuning her violin down in the shop. Finally Catterina returned to his bedside.

"Please," he said with a feeble smile, "no requiems."

She laughed. "No requiems!" I promise. I'm going to play about springtime. The first movement of Vivaldi's violin concert about the seasons of the year. This one is spring. A new beginning and the promise of wondrous things to come."

She began to play. She coaxed vibrant sonorous notes from the strings—music that filled the room with sweetness and emotion. Whether it was the special qualities of the violin or the great passion with which she played…it was of little matter. In light airy passages the notes bounced off the strings with brightness and clarity. In stronger sections she pulled from them clear, powerful, sweeping sounds.

It was as if she and her little fiddle were one. Although only a fraction of an inch smaller than the traditional size—this violin felt almost feminine in its fingering—yet it had a remarkable capacity to take bow pressure and transform it into a forceful, commanding sound.

Catterina played the Vivaldi with all the intensity and emotion of the moment. When she finally finished, she looked down at Giuseppe for the first time. His eyes were closed, and his face was serene and undisturbed. His breathing was now slow and labored. She might not have much time.

A neighbor boy was sent to fetch the parish priest. He arrived later in the evening to administer the last rites. Giuseppe had rallied somewhat but was in considerable pain. Nevertheless, he found comfort in the priest's ministrations and reassurance in his words.

"Thank you for coming, Father," said Catterina, as he prepared to leave.

"You're welcome, *Senora*. I'm glad you called for me when you did. It was good that he was lucid enough to speak with me. Sometimes…it is too late."

"Father, I know he does not have much time. The fevers have set in. I know that I will lose him, but I don't want to see him suffer so terribly."

"Whatever happens—however long— it is God's will. Your presence and loving care are his comfort. My words to you are care for him as you feel you must, and God will not fault you. I bless you my child, for your love for him. For the moment he is with you, but will soon be home with God."

The parish priest departed and Catterina returned to Giuseppe's bedside. He could not see her.

"My violins," he said in a thin voice, barely audible. "I must find my violins." His tormented body no longer had the strength to toss about. He lay there in submission on the sweat soaked bed clothes. Giuseppe looked questioningly about the room. "Where are my violins?'

Catterina held her violin in front of his face. "Here! Here is the violin. It is by far the finest one you've ever made. It has a brilliance and tonal quality that surpasses any I've ever heard."

Struggling to see, he reached out, caressing it with his fingers…running them over the newly varnished surface. Satisfied, his arm fell limply by his side. He turned to his wife. His eyes were dull and lifeless.

"Catterina," he said, in a faint whisper, "what time is it?"

"It must be several hours after midnight."

Pain and exhaustion has robbed him of any expression. He said simply, "It's your birthday."

Tears filled her eyes. Her husband had paused in dying to remember her on this day, October 17th. She realized the incredible labor of love her violin had been for him...finished in time for her birthday. She kissed his feverish forehead.

"Catterina," he whispered, "the pain, I can't bear it...please help me."

She poured a few drops of the tincture of opium into a spoon. The bottle was nearly empty. She paused...then emptied the bottle. The glistening liquid filled the little spoon—

Catterina sat at his bedside, took up her violin and began to play. She played whatever came into her head. Music she knew by memory. A fanciful combination of melodies—comic operas, lullabies, minuets, folk tunes— on she played, lost in her music.

She at last glanced at Giuseppe and stopped abruptly, her bow poised in midair. Catterina studied his chest. It was no longer heaving irregularly. It was still and his face had that certain serenity that affirmed the merciful reality.

Later that day, the following entry was penned into the church registry:

October 17, 1744

Giuseppe Guarneri, the husband of Catterina Roda,
about forty-seven years of age, having made his
confession, received Holy Viaticum & Extreme

Unction, passed away commending his soul to God.
His body to be interred in this church of S. Prospero.

Late that afternoon, the 17th of October, a young woman appeared at the doorstep of n°7 on the Piazza S. Prospero.

Catterina looked inquiringly at the plainly garbed figure standing there. "Yes? Are you looking for someone?"

"I'm looking for *Senora* Guarneri…I must speak with her."

"I am Catterina Guarneri. What is your business?"

"My name is Carlotta," said the girl nervously. "I am the one who helped your husband find the man who stabbed him. I have heard that he died. I am terribly sorry." She looked down at her feet. "I feel partly responsible for what happened. I'm sorry I ever agreed to do it." It looked now that she was about to cry. She looked Carttarina in the eyes. "I just had to come. I had to tell you this."

"Will you come in for a few minutes?"

Without a word, Carlotta accepted. They sat on stools in the workshop. The girl self-consciously looked around nervously.

"Tell me," said Catterina, "have you told this to the police?"

"No! I can't do that! The only person I've talked to...*will* talk to...is you."

"Do you have any idea where this man is now?"

"No. I don't know. He has dropped from sight."

Catterina's jaw tightened. "I wish I knew," she said, with more than a trace of anger.

"I wish I could tell you. I even talked to my uncle. He's the booking agent for the carriage line. I thought the assassin would try to leave Cremona as soon as possible, but my uncle didn't remember any one of his description."

Catterina shook her head in despair.

"He *did* recall two men who were very insistent on booking passage on yesterday's carriage to Verona, but both stages were filled...except for one seat. One of the men took that seat, the other had to wait. He is scheduled on the next carriage out—tomorrow."

"Was there none today?" asked Catterina.

"No. It leaves every other day. As you know, it's a full day to Verona, and that's as far as they go. They stay the night and return the next day....so it's every two days."

"Do you know if the man leaving tomorrow morning has baggage?"

"I asked my uncle that. He said no, he didn't pay for any baggage. But the first man—the one who left yesterday did. A trunk tied on the back."

Probably our violins, Catterina thought to herself.

"The man's name...the one leaving tomorrow, was Grimaldi. At least that's the one he gave.."

"What time do the morning stages leave?"

"At first light. Just after seven o'clock."

Catterina thanked her and acknowledged her courage in coming. When Carlotta left she was noticeably relieved, not only for the reception she received but for the opportunity to unburden herself from feelings of complicity.

Catterina sat alone in the shop. For the first time there were no violins hanging like bats from their pegs along the wall. Already the scent of fresh cut and chiseled wood was fading, and the heady odor of varnish was only faintly perceptible. She was now the sole occupant of house n° 7 on the piazza.

The young widow was not by nature a spiteful or hateful person, but she could not suppress such thoughts about the man who had killed her husband. It was constantly on her mind.

She turned to her music. It had always been a place for her to go when troubled, to get lost in her music and wander in a different place, but the violin would not take her there. When she took up her violin she played with a fury and intensity that was intoxicating—that only brought her closer to an uncontrollable desire for revenge. She knew such thoughts were not rational—even dangerous, but she could not contain her rage. Against all good judgment, she decided to see for herself if the murderous little man was, by chance, a passenger on the morning stage.

The following day, October 18th, it was still dark when Catterina hired a carriage driver to take her to the stage-coach station. Inside the carriage she jostled noisily over the cobblestones, huddled in her winter cape with Giuseppe's cane on her lap. There was no plan. She simply had to satisfy an unexplainable urge to be there—

to do *something*. She told the driver she would be seeing friends off on their journey and asked him to wait for her. Catterina fully expected that the killer would not be among the passengers, and didn't know what she would do if he was.

The station was alive with activity. Lanterns danced about like fireflies. Shouts of men pierced the air, occasionally punctuated by the whiney of an anxious horse. Baggage and freight were being lashed to the backs of carriages. Two guards, who would ride beside the driver to provide some measure of protection from highwaymen, patrolled the scene, conspicuously displaying their muskets and puffed up with self-importance. Clusters of passengers stood about, valises in hand. With her hood up, Catterina walked among them. The little man was nowhere to be seen.

As the sun began to rise on the horizon the station master shouted his instructions: "*Attenzione!* We have rules during the trip. Please do not drink on board, but if you must, be neighborly and share the bottle. Refrain from rough language if women or children are in your carriage. In the event of runaway horses stay calm and do not attempt to jump from the stage-coach. We will not be stopping for several hours. If you have to relieve yourself do so now by using one of the empty horse stalls in the stable. We will load passengers in about ten minutes."

It was then that she saw him. Maybe it was his affinity for shadows and he had been there all along, or perhaps he had just arrived. But there he was—walking toward one of the stables. Catterina was certain that he had not seen or recognized her. She followed him into the stables and passed several stalls before she saw him again.

He was standing with his back to her. She was only a few feet away when he finally turned, buttoning his pants. He glowered at her until suddenly he recognized his adversary in the dim light. The scar at the corner of his mouth pulled any expression into a leering sneer. His eyes flickered down to where Catterina had impulsively pulled off the end of the cane, exposing the thin blade of the rapier fitted into the top half. Instantly his hand slipped to his waistband.

With all her pent up wrath, Catterina lunged at the killer. The fury of her attack slammed the man backwards as the point of her weapon slipped between his ribs, penetrating to the hilt. So forceful was the assault that the blade went through his chest and into the wooden stall partition behind him.

He stood there, pinned to the wall. For a moment Catterina was paralyzed with the horror of it. Then, wrenching the rapier from his body she sheathed the bloody blade into the cane. His legs buckled and he fell to his knees.

She knew she didn't have much time. Once the boarding of the carriages began he would quickly be missed, and a search would surely follow. Hurrying to leave, she paused after a few steps and looked back. He had fallen over into the muck of the horse stall. She thought: What goes around, comes around. *"Chi la fa l'aspette!"* she yelled at him, in stinging retribution.

People were still milling about the staging area as final preparations for departure were completed. Her driver, waiting some distance away, helped her into the carriage and, after a few clucks and a shake of the reins, his horse began clopping back to house nº 7 on the Pizza S. Prospero.

The rhythmic clop of the horse's hooves closely matched the pounding in her chest. Her mind was a tangle of conflict. Catterina was shocked and greatly disturbed by what she had done, but strangely not remorseful. She wasn't sure it was an act of self-defense or she had simply taken advantage of the circumstances. Moreover, she wasn't even certain of her real motive in coming here. Perhaps if she could get past that, she could say it was truly self-defense. Or was it really?

Chapter Four

A week passed when an Austrian officer appeared at the doorstep of n° 7. *Oberleutnant* Stefan Horak was paying Catterina an official call.

At once she found him handsome in his own way, and resplendent in his uniform. After exchanging pleasantries he came to the point.

"*Senora,* first of all, my condolences on the death of your husband at the hands of an unknown assailant. Ah...never having been married myself, I cannot imagine such a loss. This tragedy must be compounded by the robbery of your shop the day before. But this is not the primary reason for my visit…"

Catterina shifted uneasily in her chair. This man had a certain air about him, a manner which was direct, but nevertheless reassuring and non-threatening.

"I have been assigned to investigate a murder. The murder of a man at the stage-coach station. The local police have asked us for our assistance." He smiled, "It seems in difficult cases they are quite willing to admit their own inadequacy. In any event, our garrison is here to protect the area and maintain law and order—so we are happy to oblige."

"Who is this man?" Catterina asked cautiously.

"We don't really know. The name he gave was a false one and he had no identity papers. We only know he was not from this area."

"Who does not carry identity papers?" she probed.

"Precisely. Someone who does not want to be known," he replied. "It appears he may match the description of someone who robbed your shop, along with several other shopkeepers. He had rather distinctive physical characteristics, so I am inclined to believe it's the same man. I am wondering if you can describe him for me?"

"A small man—short. Hard, with a scar on his chin."

"Yes," he said thoughtfully. "Was your husband ever able to describe the man who attacked him?"

"No. He said it was very dark. It could have been this man…he only said he was rather small."

"Very well, then. Oh, just one more thing, *Senora* Guarneri. The morning this man was killed, October 18th, were you home?"

"Yes, I was home. Home alone…which I suppose I must now get used to."

"I thought so. The person that killed this man must have been very strong. It was a very violent, vicious murder."

A chill ran down Catterina's spine.

"The natural inclination." he continued, "is to assume that the robberies and the two murders within three days are somehow connected. However sometimes it can just be a coincidence and perhaps that may be what it is in this case. Thank you for your time, *Senora.*" He rose to go. "If I may ask you one more question…I hope you don't think me impertinent."

She looked at him warily.

"You don't appear to be Italian—Nordic perhaps?"

She laughed with relief. "I was born in the Tyrol. As a girl I studied music in Saltsburg."

"You are Austrian then?"

"Ja, en Österreighisches Mädchen."

"You are! I myself am from a little farm near Bischofshofen!"

Catterina was beginning to feel a bit more comfortable.

"Well, then," he said, attempting to regain a military bearing, "I won't trouble you more. If I have any further questions I hope you will allow me to return."

She knew he would, and she hoped it would not be on official business.

Oberleutnant Horak *did* come back. At first it was with feeble excuses pursuant to the investigation, but as time passed they became so transparent that he dropped them altogether. A strong relationship began to develop between these two displaced Austrians. Happiness began to slowly creep back into Catterina's life.

Chapter Five

Strangely, Catterina felt no remorse for killing the murderous little thief and guilt only to the extent she was surprised that she was capable of such a thing. A few weeks later she began to venture out on her regular trips to the market. Time had begun to loosen tragedy's grip on her life.

She stopped at the baker's shop and then headed down the street to the butcher before returning home. Meat, even that of very poor quality, was a luxury for most people and Catterina only occasionally could afford the expenditure.

The butcher was an honest man and had a son who, at that time, was called "feeble minded" but was in fact only moderately impaired. The boy was quite large for his age and towered over most men but was gentle and trusting by nature. He spent most of his day selling and wrapping meat in his father's shop.

He always brightened whenever Catterina entered the shop. She treated him with respect and went out of her way to engage him in conversation and as a result he always tried to select the better cuts of meat for her, sometimes disappearing into the back of the shop to bring out fresher meat.

Catterina stepped into the shop and was immediately met with a broad grin from the butcher's son.

"*Ciao, signora* Guarnari!"

"*Ciao,* Marcello. I haven't been in for a while. It's so good to see you. What do you have today—anything special?"

"We have some lamb cuts in the back. It was butchered only three days ago."

"That sounds nice, but just one. I'm alone now you know."

The familiar smile momentarily evaporated. "Yes. I know. That was a bad man to do that."

Marcello lumbered into the back room as Catterina glanced at the dozen or so hunks of meat lying on a wooden table in the open air of the shop. The boy-man returned accompanied by his portly father.

"I'm sorry about your husband, *senora*," said the father, wiping his hands on a bloody apron. "Except for your grief I hope you are well.."

"It's getting a bit easier," replied Catterina. "At first I wasn't sure, but I have decided to go ahead and play with my music ensemble at our concert this week."

"Oh, please—can I go?" pleaded Marcello to his father. "You can take the money out of my allowance," he begged.

"We'll see…" said the father patting him affectionately on the shoulder, "we'll see."

Catterina turned to leave and Marcello rushed to open the door.

"Thank you, Marcello. "You are very kind."

An unabashed grin accompanied his rapidly nodding head.

†

Catterina *did* play with the little orchestra of local musicians, for despite the loss of Giuseppe she could not resist the opportunity to play on her new, very own violin. Cremona, as most towns its size, did not have a professional orchestra of its own and these loosely organized musical societies were common and often the only exposure the local populace had to concert music.

The concert was held in an old parish church near the north wall of the city. In the winter season it was always cold in the rough stone and polished marble interiors of these churches and the audience as well as the orchestra sprouted an odd assemblage of scarfs, sweaters, jackets and even a few coats. Conspicuous among the audience was a man who sat alone and was dressed in a manner that would attract attention anywhere in the streets of a provincial town like Cremona. The young man wore a long narrow coat trimmed in gold braid over an embroidered shirt with ruffles. His trousers were knee length tied with ribbons and his shoes adorned with silver buckles. Even in the large cities he would likely be considered overdressed. Some would think him a dandy.

The orchestra played a variety of selections of Mozart and Boccherini. Catterina soon became lost in her music. On this violin she had never played better. She did not see the stranger in the audience and could not know what implications his presence would have on her life.

†

The strange man in the crowd was Alexandro Luppucci and a favorite of a titular bishop in the region. This bishop served under the direction of the bishop of the diocese as he had been reprimanded and reduced to a titular bishop for a variety of transgressions. Among them was misappropriation of church funds and property for personal use, along with "a possible tendency toward licentious behavior". It was widely assumed that Rome might well have overlooked such activities, but he also had strong Jesuit leanings and as a result he had been put under the supervision of a traditionalist bishop. Predictably, the arrangement did not work well and the two men could barely tolerate each other.

The morning after the concert Alexandro could hardly wait to see the titular bishop. He was a man on a mission and fully intended to use his influence on the older man to his advantage,

Alexandro struck a pose as the bishop entered the room.

"Ah, Alexandro, you are in a merry spirit this morning!"

"Good sir, your presence provokes such a mood."

"I'm told you were waiting to see me."

Alexandro slipped his arm around the bishop's waist and drew him aside. "Last night—on a whim, mind you—I attended a little concert at the church of S. Agostino. The music was a bit average for my taste but one instrument stood out." His eyes flashed and he gave a little quiver of excitement. "It was an attractive middle-aged woman playing a violin..."

The bishop interrupted "My dear Alexandro, when did an attractive woman ever receive your attention?"

"Stop! I'm serious. It wasn't the woman, it was the *violin*. Oh, she played exceptionally well—but it was the sounds she coaxed out of it...sounds purer and sweeter than I have ever heard. It had a rich deep sound and yet bright and vigorous. It was incredible!"

"Well, I'm glad you enjoyed it."

"No, you don't understand," pleaded Alexandro "I *want* that violin. More than anything in the world I want it!"

Alexandro had grown up getting what he wanted. He was the son of a wealthy merchant in Lombardi who had a remote family connection to the House of Modena. Alexandro lived extravagantly and had never held any position that provided income for him, and as a result his father had cut him off except for a trust fund which nevertheless regularly paid a handsome sum. Of course it was not enough.

The bishop looked inquisitively at his companion. "So—you want this violin. Why are you telling me this?"

"Because I know you can get it for me. You have your ways...unless," he pursed his lips into a pout "you don't want to."

Alexandro was, in fact, right and he knew it. The titular bishop had a long history of getting what he wished by whatever means. True, he was now officially under the control of the regional bishop but he was feeling embolden because of recent events. A few months before, on September 22, 1774, Pope Clement XIV died suddenly at the age of sixty-eight. A conclave was convened to replace the traditionalist pope but no consensus had been reached as the Jesuits had many adherents in the Roman Curia and the College of Cardinals.

"Who was this woman with the violin?" asked the bishop.

In the program she was listed as Catterina Roda Guarneri."

"Ah, Guiseppe's wife. He was murdered by an unknown person little more than a month ago. He will be making no more violins."

"I want *that* violin. *Her* violin. I would never forget this kindness. It would be a gift that I would treasure in my heart forever."

"I'm sure," replied the bishop with resignation, for he knew he had a problem. He harbored a special affection for this young man. He knew it was not a wise thing to do but he felt compelled to whatever was necessary to stay in the favor and good grace of the young man. "I can't promise anything but I'll see what I can do. Will you come back to Cremona and visit me soon?"

"You know I can't stay away for long," the young man replied.

†

An emissary from the bishop was sent to the house at no. 7 S. Prospero to acquire the violin from Catterina Guarneri. An enormous sum was offered but she flatly refused to part with the violin her husband, at the end of his life, had lovingly made for her.

The bishop was furious and so he turned to his nefarious connections both inside and outside the law.

The Prefect for the Enforcement of Law, Order and Security rose from his desk as the bishop entered. The head of police in Cremona was an official looking man with a wide blue sash spread boldly across his chest. On his desk were an assortment of stamps, seals and important appearing papers scattered about. A tri-cornered hat with a few tattered feathers sat conspicuously on a corner of the official's desk.

"My dear bishop, what brings you down from your heavenly position to the depths of my unsavory world?" he said, offering the bishop a seat.

"I was hoping you might be able to help me with a certain matter of concern to me. I am saddened by the recent murders in our city...two within three days of each other. It occurs to me that here might be some connection of sorts and I wonder if there is any information you might be able to share with me?"

The officer cleared his throat. "Of course we thought of a possible connection. I have asked the local militia for assistance and they have assigned an officer from the garrison to investigate, but unfortunately neither of us has been able to turn up any leads. There is not much I can tell you."

The bishop stood and began pacing for effect. "Let me get right to the point." He stopped and turned to the officer. "Doesn't it occur to you that the murdered man's wife might be a suspect in the second murder—especially if it was known she was at the scene of the crime?"

The officer's eyes grew wide. "But,...but..." he stuttered, "how do you know that?"

"You know I can't reveal what I learn in the course of my administering to the flock. I counsel, placate and hear their concerns in strict confidence and anonymity." The bishop approached the gaping officer. "But I can tell you this'" he said looking heavenward, "there is a carriage driver who drove the person in question to the station that morning. You may want to speak with him. His name is Benito Sarto."

"Sarto!' exclaimed the officer. "Yes. We know him. A troublesome sort."

It was no surprise that that Benito Sarto was known to the law for he was just the kind of man who would take a bribe in exchange for false testimony. The bishop had, in fact, no idea that Catterina was in any way involved in the little assassin's death but he wanted to place her at the carriage station the morning the man was stabbed, and to do that he needed to find someone who was willing to falsely testify that she was there. It was some distance from the house at no. 7 to the assembly station and, especially in the early morning hours, a woman would certainly have taken a carriage...who better then, thought the bishop, than a driver who was willing to say he drove her there. Sarto was a petty thief and a small time career criminal—willing to do just about anything for a few lire. An emissary of the bishop had made the necessary arrangements with the man.

The grateful officer nearly fell over himself thanking his visitor, vowing that he would look into the matter at once.

The bishop was pleased and smug. His plan was now in motion.

†

Only a few days passed before two policemen appeared unannounced at Catterina's door. She was arrested on suspicion of murder and taken to the old city jail. As might be expected it was dreary place, dark and cold. Catterina was both surprised and terrified, and the brooding question on her mind was what possible evidence did they have for her arrest. She had been confident that no one had recognized her and she had been merely an obscure figure in the crowd at the carriage station. It had been a cold predawn morning and, as had most women and a few men, worn a hooded cloak which would have made it nearly impossible to be clearly seen.

Hours passed. She sat in her cell, knees drawn up and huddled against the chill. Then, there was a scurry of activity and muffled voices. A key turned in the lock shattering the silence and a jailer dutifully stood aside as the bishop, frock flowing, swept into the cell. Catterina had never met the bishop and knew little about him and was surprised that a man of such eminence stood in the gloom of her little cell.

"I am deeply sorry to see you in such an unpleasant situation, *senora*. I have come to see if there is something that I can do to help you."

For a moment Catterina was startled—then blurted the first thing to come to her mind. "Yes, get me out of here. I don't belong here."

"That may well be, my dear child, but I can't have the charges against you dismissed. What I can perhaps do is get you out of this miserable place on bail, but it will require a substantial amount of money. After all, you have been arrested for murder."

"I don't understand—"

"My dear, I am prepared to post the bail for your release. Is that something you would like me to do?"

"Oh yes—if you would be so kind!"

In the darkness of the cell the bishop smiled a cruel smile. "It *is* out of kindness and compassion that I do this for you but you must understand that I cannot do this without some assurance that I am not risking the church's money. Is there something of value that you can give me in return...something as surety until bail is no longer required?"

Catterina lowered her eyes. "I'm not a wealthy woman and now with my husband gone little means of support. I don't know what I might give you of any value," she said thoughtfully, "...except a little necklace my family once gave me. It has a little emerald and some small rubies and diamonds," she said plaintively. "They're all quite small—but you could have that."

"No, I'm afraid that wouldn't quite do. He rubbed his chin in thought. "Your husband was a luthier...perhaps I *could* take some violins."

Her heart sank. "They were all stolen by the thieves. We have nothing."

"I see," said the bishop "well I was hoping..." He started to leave, then turned back. "Do you not have a single violin left?"

"Just my violin. One that my husband made for me."

"Well then" said the bishop hesitantly, "it isn't much—but I suppose it will have to do." He smiled but it was lost in the dimness. "I'll make the arrangements then. I expect I'll have you out of here by morning."

†

She was mending clothes upstairs in the house at no. 7. Needle in hand she paused and looked up. The knocking on the downstairs door became louder but she wasn't sure she wanted to answer it. She had been released from prison only that morning and she was in no mood to see anyone.

The knocking became more insistent and with a sigh of resignation she went to the window. Standing below, resplendent in his uniform, was Austrian army officer *Oberleutnant* Steffan Horak. Spontaneously she drew in a little breath. The officer wore a maroon tailcoat emblazoned with a bright yellow sash and white trousers tucked into black calf-length boots. A broad-billed hat was festooned with a little red plume. He indeed cut a handsome figure.

Catterina hurried downstairs smoothing her dress and tucking errant wisps of hair under her cap.

"Catterina!" he exclaimed when he saw her. "I wonder if I might come in."

The informality at once put her at ease. "Please come in my dear *Oberleutnant*."

He came right to the point. "I just heard that you had been arrested and had to spend the night in jail. It is a dismal place and I can't bear the thought of you there. They said you had been released and I came here as soon as I could."

Catterina cringed, twisting her hands in her lap. "It was horrible—like a bad dream. I just don't understand it all."

"Let me tell you what I know. Apparently a man—a carriage driver—has come forward claiming that he remembers driving you to the carriage station the morning that the unidentified man was killed. On the strength of his testimony the police arrested you pending a preliminary hearing. My garrison commander is quite annoyed because the police had asked us for assistance but failed to tell us anything about this."

"How could this driver possibly identify me...if I wasn't there?"

"I don't know Catterina but I am going to find out—I promise you. Trust me. We know that this driver is somewhat of an unsavory character and has been in trouble with the law numerous times. There *should* be some question as to how much he can be trusted but the police apparently believed him."

Catterina looked sad and frightened. "Oh, Steffan, what should I do? Do I need to find a lawyer?"

"No, not now."

"Good. I have little money for a lawyer and I've already had to give up my violin—the one Giuseppe made for me."

Steffan frowned. "But why have you had to give up your violin?"

"The bishop. The bishop came to see me in my cell. He told me he could get me out on bail if I would give him the violin as security for paying my bail."

Stefan was silent, the frown still on his face. Finally he said "I see. Catterina let me ask you, if you were to go out in the chill of the morning what would you wear?"

"Well—my wool cloak."

"Does it have a hood?"

"A big hood."

"What color is it?"

"Why, it's grey. Grey with silver clasps."

Stefan rose to go, taking her hands in his. His hands were warm, rough and comforting. "Don't you worry. I have been assigned as the investigator for our garrison and I promise you I will get to the bottom of this."

A little chill ran up her spine and they said goodbye.

†

Stefan headed straight for the police station where he had persuaded them to bring back the carriage driver for further questioning.

Carlos Santos was a swarthy man and a cocky sort but the *Oberleutnant* thought he detected a trace of uneasiness under the brash exterior.

"The *Oberleutnant* is working with us on this murder case," explained one of the police officers "he would like to ask you a few questions if you don't mind."

Perhaps it was Steffan's impressive uniform or maybe that the Austrian military had been brought into the case—but Santos shifted nervously in his chair, eyes darting apprehensively.

Stefan flashed a disarming smile. "You said that you were the driver who picked up a woman at no.7 S. Prospero very early in the morning of October nineteenth and drove her to the carriage station, is this correct?"

"Yes, sir."

Stefan looked puzzled. "This woman—I would like to know more about this woman."

"She was the woman whose husband was killed two days before."

"How do you know this?"

"Because she lived at house no.7 on the piazza and that is where I picked her up."

"Who told you this woman lived there and she needed a carriage that morning?"

Santos hesitated. "I don't remember."

"But someone must have told you she wanted a carriage and to go to the station. I would like to talk to this person."

"I just...don't remember who it was."

"I see," said Steffan "and what did this woman look like?"

"She had blond hair and a pale complexion."

"And what was she wearing?"

"A coat—a coat down to her ankles."

"Can you describe this coat for me?"

"Well—it was a heavy coat."

"Do you remember what color it was?"

He hesitated. "Brown."

"Light brown or dark brown?"

"Medium brown."

"All right. Now was this a coat or a cloak?"

The carriage driver sensed trouble. "It *could* have been a cloak—I couldn't see that clearly."

"But you saw it clearly enough to know it was brown...a medium brown—"

"Well, yes."

"Now, *Senore* Santos, all women's cloaks and most long coats have hoods. Did this cloak...or coat...you're not sure, have a hood?"

"Yes."

"And what time of morning did you say you drove her to the station and back?"

"Dark when I picked her up and twilight and just beginning to dawn when I drove her back."

"Hmm, that morning, the nineteenth of October was overcast and foggy. Do you remember that?"

"Yes, of course."

"I'm puzzled, *Senore* Santos. Since it was dark or just beginning to get light...and foggy...and she was wearing a hood, how could you see the color of her hair, let alone her complexion?"

Santos waved his arms helplessly in the air. "Of course I can't be certain. I can't be sure of *everything*! But I did pick her up at that address."

"Look here," said Stefan sternly "you *may* have picked *someone* up on that street, although I doubt it, but it certainly wasn't *Senora* Guarneri. She doesn't have a brown coat or cloak...or whatever you say you saw. I think, *Senore* Santos, that you are getting way in over your head and the only way out for you is to tell the truth. If not, with your record there will be no leniency. I don't think you want to go to prison again. Now—and I want you to think about this before you answer—who told you that *Senora* Guarneri had blond hair and a fair complexion...because you certainly couldn't have seen this that morning."

Santos sat in silence, obviously weighing his options. "I don't know. Honestly I don't know. I only know what the man said...that it was the bishop who told him."

One of the policemen drew a quick gasp. The other looked on wide-eyed.

Santos reacted immediately. "No—not our bishop—it was the *other* one."

"The *titular* bishop?" asked Stefan.

"That's the one. But I never spoke with him. That's just what I was told."

"Who told you?"

"The go-between, and I don't even know his name—he was careful about that."

"Thank you, *Senore* Santos. Just to be clear: You were paid to make this story up and you did?"

The man hung his head. "Yes," he said quietly.

One of the police officers led Carlos Santos away. The other shook his head in disbelief—"But," said the officer "it was the bishop who asked permission to see her in her cell, and then put up her bail..."

"Yes, I know, and in exchange he forced her to put up one of her few possessions as surety—her violin."

"How do you know this?" asked the policeman incredulously.

"Sir", said Stefan with a touch of sarcasm "you asked the militia for help in this investigation. I just did my job."

†

The wheels of Italian justice turn slowly but eventually all charges were dropped against Catterina. She was, of course, much relieved that her whereabouts that fateful morning were not revealed. The whole incident strengthened her attraction to this Austrian artillery officer who had come to her aid.

Unfortunately one problem remained. Although there was no longer a need for bail the violin had not been returned to Catterina. She had tried of course, but was unable to make any contact with the bishop. He was unavailable to see her and when she left notes with his office or housekeeper they were ignored. In desperation she turned to Stefan although she couldn't imagine what he could possibly do.

†

There were those in Cremona who knew of the bishop's devious behavior and questionable reputation. No one knew all the details—but there was ample amount to make for lively gossip and a steady supply of facts, rumors and innuendos. There were always a few who refused to believe that such an elevated man of the cloth could possibly be guilty of such improprieties. Then, like Catterina, there was a segment of the populace who either didn't care or were not generally in a position to hear such things.

It was now mid-November. Every day, unless the weather was bad, was market day for Catterina. This morning she made her rounds, stopping at the bakers for bread then on to the vegetable stalls to see what might have come in from the fields. As usual the last stop was the butcher shop.

The butcher's son brightened the moment he saw her. "*Senora* Guarneri!" he said greeting her with a series of little bows.

"Marcello, what do you have for me today?"

"Not much. We plan to have a lamb to butcher tomorrow. I feel bad to tell you this. You are a nice person—you are my favorite person!"

"Please don't feel bad. You are my favorite person too,"

"It was not nice to put you in jail" said the boy. "I didn't like it when they did that."

It was a mistake, Marcello, so let's just forget about it."

"Will you be playing in a concert again? I didn't get to go last time you played."

"I'm afraid I don't know. I lost my violin."

Marcello frowned. "Where did you lose it...maybe I can help find it?"

"No, it's a long story—the bishop has it and won't give it back."

The boy's eyes widened, then narrowed and his jaw tightened. "The *bad* bishop? He's not a nice man."

Catterina laughed. "How do you know he's bad?"

"Bonita. She buys meat from me and she's my friend. Bonita is a housekeeper and cook for the bishop and he is mean to her. He calls her bad names and says she never does anything right. He says she will always be a bad girl—and he hurts her." Marcello's fists were tight and his face flushed with anger. "Her family is poor and arranged for her to work for him. She had a little room there and has to work hard every day. She says she's going to leave some day but I don't know where she would go,"

The butcher came out of the back room and looked inquisitively at his son. "I heard voices but I don't see that anything has been sold," he chuckled.

"I stopped in to see if you had anything new," said Catterina "Marcello tells me you will be getting a lamb in. I'll be back again tomorrow after you butcher."

A customer entered and the butcher turned his attention to the woman. Catterina thanked the boy, left the shop and continued home.

†

Pen in hand the bishop sat at his writing desk, took out a sheet of his personal stationary, and began scratching a letter to Alexandro Luppucci:

22 November 1774
My Dearest Alexandro,

You will no doubt be pleased to learn that I have acquired your coveted violin. After considerable expense and effort it is now in my possession and awaits your return to Cremona to fetch it.

Alas, since my youth I have never been blessed with a delicate appreciation of music and I must confess I fail to understand your fascination with this fiddle. Nevertheless I have it here and I urge you in the strongest terms to come as soon as possible and take it away from here and back to Milan. I must be able to say that the violin is no longer in my possession, has disappeared, and I have no knowledge of where it might be.

Perhaps you might play this violin for me when you come here. Although I may not be able to appreciate the melody to the fullest, your sweet voice will be music to my heart and ample reward...

A timid knock at the door interrupted the bishop. "Yes, what is it?" he said harshly.

The young housekeeper appeared in the doorway. "Pardon, but I wanted you to know that lunch is ready," said the girl. "It's chowder and I know you dislike it when it's cold."

"Very well!" said the bishop laying his pen aside. "I am nearly finished with a letter which I want you to post on the next coach to Milan. Do you think you can be trusted with that?"

"Yes, sir," she replied with eyes lowered.

Clam chowder was one of the bishop's favorite soups and he ate heartily, dipping his bread and slurping from his spoon until it was more than nearly half gone. Suddenly he felt a bit dizzy. Then the room began to spin. He was breathing heavily now and struggling to catch his breath. He tried to call out to the housekeeper but no words would come. His face was crimson and he was sweating profusely. The bishop attempted to stand but slumped back in his chair. Then, he pitched forward—his face into the half eaten bowl.

†

An investigation was launched, of sorts, but no one seemed to want to pursue the bishop's mysterious death. The church was uncomfortable with what his past behavior might disclose and seemed to prefer that the whole incident would quietly fade away. It was widely known that the bishop had many enemies and despised by any number of them who would have pleased with his demise. His young housekeeper had left and the girl could not be located. His cause of death was initially determined to be the result of poisoning from an unknown substance, but later it was pronounced that it was probably "excesses and over exertion of a weak heart"...and everyone seemed satisfied with that.

Curiously, now every time Catterina entered the butcher's shop Marcello would greet her with "Do you have your violin back yet?"

"No," she would reply and the boy would grin sheepishly and change the subject.

A week passed when the local police received an anonymous envelope containing the bishop's letter to Alexandro. Although unsigned, it was recognized as the bishop's handwriting as well as on his personal stationary. A crude note was attached:

Tis violn belongs to Senora Gaurneri. It were taken from her. She has tryd to get it back.

Oberleutnant Horak was shown the envelope and its contents and quickly confirmed that the violin had been given up as surety for Catterina's bail and since all charges had been dismissed the violin should have been returned. Escorted by several police officers he entered the bishop's residence, recovered the violin, and personally returned it to Catterina.

She was, of course, delighted and was more than happy to credit her handsome *Oberleutnant* in once again coming to her aid.

And Marcello? He danced a childish little jig the day he learned her violin had been returned. His father, the butcher, took him to Catterina's next concert and he smiled proudly as he watched her playing with the little violin cradled affectionately against her cheek. He knew people didn't consider him a bright boy but maybe...just maybe, he wasn't as dumb as they thought.

†

From here on the story grows cold... hereafter, little is known about Catterina and her violin. Her relationship with the dashing Austrian officer continued until his regiment received notice that it would be recalled to Austria, and with the impending relocation Catterina and Stefan decided to marry.

She was married on April 28, 1748, to infantry officer *Oberleutnant* Stefan Horak. Her name now reflected her Austrian heritage—once again she was Katarina...Katarina Horak.

She left Cremona with her husband and her most cherished possession—never to return to Italy. Katarina lived out her life somewhere in Austria, doubtless her little violin never far from her side...

ROBERT MITCHELL

Part Two

ROBERT MITCHELL

Chapter Six

Professor Kendall Campbell looked up from his work and listened intently. He had gone back to his office at Boston University to grade student papers. The building was in a quiet corner of the campus where there were no evening classes or student activities. It was a good time for the associate professor to escape the clamor and interruptions of the school day.

He was about to return to his work when his office door burst open. The professor whirled around in his chair as a figure raced toward him.

"Daddy!" she cried, as his daughter flung her arms around him. Kathleen Campbell was twenty-three, but she still called him "daddy"—an expression of endearment he was quite fond of. Along with his undergraduate teaching, she was his world.

Three years earlier his wife left him and married a Hollywood entertainment agent. She had never been satisfied as the wife of an art history teacher and she considered it rather stuffy and boring. Moreover, financially it did not allow the lifestyle she craved. Now she had a Beverly Hills address and she could shop Rodeo Drive whenever she wished. Kendall hoped she was happy, but he doubted it.

"Kathleen!" He held her at arm's length. "You scared me. I didn't know the building was still open. What are you doing here?"

Her face flushed with excitement. "I just had to come over and tell you. I first went to the apartment, and when you weren't there I knew you must be working late." A huge smile filled her face. "I've been selected to play in the exchange program in France."

Kendall pulled up a chair. "Sit down. Tell me all about it."

'It's a string chamber ensemble...all from northeastern schools. The cellist is from Berklee, the viola is a guy at Temple. I'm representing Amherst, and the other violin—I think she is a grad student at Syracuse. That's our quartet!"

"When's the concert?"

"Not until April. Late April, I think. In the south of France—in Nice, actually. I want you there. I so hope you can come."

"Of course I'll be there. I'll talk to the dean tomorrow."

Kathleen gushed on. "The French ensemble has their concert before ours...in New York in January. I volunteered to be their exchange host while they are here."

"What music will you play?"

"It hasn't been chosen yet. I hope they do soon. I want to start practicing."

Kendall rose and put his hand on her shoulder. "When your mother and I sent you to the music conservatory each summer...I knew then that your passion for music and love of the violin would become an important part of your life. Now," he said, stuffing papers into his desk, "I don't think you should go back up to Amherst tonight. Stay here in Boston. We can grab something to eat on the way back to my apartment."

Kathleen did stay in the city that night. They stopped at a little restaurant, ate pizza and drank beer from the bottle.

The proud father and elated daughter toasted the occasion with a click of their bottles. They could not know that an unfamiliar and dangerous world of conspiracy and intrigue was about to snare them it its web.

ROBERT MITCHELL

Chapter Seven

In late January in New York City, an airport shuttle van pulled in front of the Ritz-Carleton Hotel on Central Park South. A doorman hurried to assist the five passengers. A quartet of French music students and their director had arrived for a concert at Lincoln Center.

A few blocks away, their American host had already checked in at the Empire Hotel on West 63rd

Street. The American planning committee had booked Kathleen into the Empire, rather than with the French at the Ritz-Carleton. Why, she didn't know, perhaps for reasons of economy—maybe availability. It didn't much matter. They were within walking distance of each other.

She was by nature a trusting young woman, Kathleen. Maybe even a little naïve. Her father always said she wore her feelings on her sleeve, but for the most part it was a refreshing and engaging expression of who she was.

A welcoming dinner was planned for the visiting French, with Kathleen as their host. Then tomorrow she would escort them to the concert hall for an afternoon rehearsal, followed by the evening performance. The following two days were free for the French musicians to explore New York on their own before returning home. At least that was the plan.

It was an hour and half before Kathleen would meet the group and escort them to dinner. She found a quiet, unoccupied alcove off her hotel lobby to kill some time before the walk to the Ritz-Carleton. It was a secluded area except for two men seated nearby and an occasional passerby. For a time her mind wandered over the good fortune that had brought her here. Then, with little more than idle curiosity, her attention turned to the two men partially obstructed by a potted palm.

They appeared an unlikely pair. One seemed to be a business man, well dressed, with a serious almost severe demeanor. The other was casually dressed in sneakers, athletic pants and a hooded jacket, and appeared to be Hispanic. With little else to do, Kathleen continued to watch them. They appeared to be engaged in an earnest conversation of some importance.

It happed so fast she wasn't all certain of what she saw, but something seemed to pass between them. The businessman's arm crossed the table, and as it did his arm extended beyond his sleeve to reveal an indigo bracelet— no a tattoo perhaps, of what looked like an intricate pattern of intertwined spears or pitchforks. An unusual design, she thought. Then, in a few seconds, it disappeared as his wrist withdrew into his sleeve.

Kathleen's cell phone jangled.

"Hi honey. It's Dad...just wanted to know if you've checked in."

"I'm at my hotel now. I'm just about to walk over and take them to dinner."

"Ok. Be careful. Love you..."

"Love you too." She snapped the cover on her phone and looked up. The men were gone—time to meet the French.

She found them waiting in the lobby. The director, Madame Trubault, made introductions: "This is Paulette Séverin...Margaux Cousineau...and then our two men, Henri Patenaude...and Pepe Benedetti." Kathleen was surprised when the French women each embraced her adding a a peck on each cheek. When it came to the men, Henri took her hand and pretentiously kissed it. "We are French, no? You must expect no less," he said with a broad smile, accompanied by laughter from the women.

Not to be outdone, Pepe did the same. "Henri sets a standard of behavior I am most willing to follow," he said gallantly.

Kathleen was never one for first impressions, but she couldn't help but like this group. She passed out a schedule for the next day including the arrival time of the van to take them to the concert hall. "Tonight we are going to welcome you to New York with dinner at a restaurant on Central Park South. It's only about three or four blocks from here, and since it's unseasonably warm for this time of year we'll walk if you don't mind. I will be your host while you are here, so if there is anything you need you will find my hotel and phone number on your schedule. Now—I know that dinner tonight is earlier than you are accustomed, but we are Americans, no? You must expect no less." She laughed, along with the French. "Now, if you will follow me—"

Kathleen and Madame Tribault walked ahead, followed by Paulette and Henri engaged in a lively conversation. Some distance behind were Margaux and Pepe—Kathleen wondered if they were a couple.

It was an upscale Italian restaurant. It would have been much too pretentious to take them to a French one. They had a table off to the side. Intentional or not, Pepe sat next to Kathleen, with Madame Tribault on the other side. Margaux ended up seated on the opposite side of the table and did not seem too happy about it. It obviously made her uncomfortable.

The sommelier had been informed that this table had some budget limitations and he obliged with appropriate recommendations from his wine list. Once, during dinner, Kathleen's napkin slipped to the floor. When she attempted to retrieve it she was met with a wave of Pepe's hand.

"Allow me, *mon cher*, I'll get it," he said as he pushed back his chair.

Kathleen thought she might have sensed a certain tone to his voice—an attentiveness, that...but maybe it was just characteristic of Frenchmen. What she didn't know, and perhaps might have realized, Pepe Benedetti was not French.

By the time they left the restaurant Kathleen and Pepe were deeply engaged in conversation, and as the group made its way back to the hotel the two lagged behind. If it was obvious to others—and to Margaux, Kathleen and Pepe didn't seem to care. They missed a street light and fell further behind. Ahead, the rest of the group finally fell out of sight.

"My family is very supportive of my interest in music," he said. "I'm not a great cellist. Maybe good, but not great. I was really surprised when I was selected for this concert in America."

"Have you been here before?"

"Oh, no, I've never been outside of Europe." They walked in silence before he spoke again, "Now enough of me, let's talk about you. "How did you—"

It happened so fast that it took them by complete surprise. Out of nowhere three young men appeared, surrounding them. Without a word they began to beat and pummel Pepe.

Kathleen cried out in disbelief. "What are you doing! What do you want? "

As two of the men restrained him, the other hit Pepe hard in the stomach and he doubled over and fell to the sidewalk. Kathleen flung herself at the man and he turned, knocking her to the ground. They all began to kick Pepe savagely...then the flash of a knife blade appeared in the hand of one of them. He stepped toward Pepe waving it wildly. *"No mas!"* commanded one of the men, and as quickly as they had appeared they ran and disappeared around the corner.

Cars and taxis continued to pass by as if the incident had never occurred. She helped him as he struggled to his feet. A passerby paused to ask if they were all right, then continued on his way.

Kathleen was frantic. "Are you OK? Are you hurt badly?"

Pepe responded with a grimace. "It's all right," he said breathlessly. Blood curled down from his nose. "I'm all right, really."

She took out her cell phone and flipped open the cover.

"What are you doing?" he said, grabbing her arm.

"Calling the police."

"No! Don't call the police," he said firmly. "Trust me Kathleen. You must trust me. We just need to get back to the hotel."

She took him by the arm and they slowly made their way back to the Ritz-Carleton. Over Kathleen's protestations he insisted that she take a taxi back to her hotel. As she was about to enter the cab she felt his hand gently on her shoulder. She turned, and without warning he kissed her.

"Thank you," he said, "for a quite eventful evening. It was a brave thing you did. You could have been hurt. Please—let this be our secret. I don't want the director or my ensemble to know about it."

"Why?"

"You have to trust me," was all he said.

The taxi pulled away from the curb and she looked back to see him limping into the hotel. In the confinement of the cab Kathleen sat shaken and confused. She knew she would call her father as soon as she was back in her room. She could not know that Pepe was already talking to his.

The next day Kathleen could hardly wait to see him. When she arrived in a van to pick up the French ensemble for rehearsal they were waiting in the lobby, a pile of black instrument cases at their feet. Her eyes searched the group for Pepe. He was looking directly at her. She quickly looked away...

Clearly musicians had not anticipated the enormity of the Lincoln Center complex. Expressions of "*C'est magnifique!*" and "*Trés impressionant!*" spilled from the group, heads twisting about. Kathleen escorted Madame Trabault as they led the way to the performance hall. It was comfortable, but not elegant, and acoustically as intimate as the venue itself. The music hall had a small stage and only accommodated several hundred seats. The ensemble began unpacking their instruments and setting up as Kathleen searched backstage for a chair. She would watch the rehearsal from the wings.

It was then she felt Pepe's hand on her shoulder and heard his soft voice.

"I must see you, Kathleen."

She looked up inquiringly.

"It will be difficult without being known by the others, but it is important that I see you alone. Must go. Talk to you later," he said, leaving with his cello in hand and a noticeable limp.

Kathleen watched and listened intently as Madame Trabault led the chamber orchestra through a brisk rehearsal, stopping only once or twice to finesse a passage. Even from her position off stage Kathleen could see the faint crescent of a bruise under Pepes' eye. She wondered how he had explained it to his French companions. His fingering and bowing appeared unaffected—as much as she could tell. However, she saw him unconsciously rub his shoulder from time to time. Occasionally Kathleen caught Margaux looking impassively in her direction.

The French quartet was both talented and well-rehearsed. Madame Trabault ended the session assuring them that the evening would be a *"concert extraordinaire"*.

It was indeed. Kathleen sat in the second row of a sold out house. Many seats were occupied by French compatriots eager to support their quartet from the South of France.

Madame Trabault took the stage for the introduction: *"Bonsior, mesdames et messieurs*—good evening, ladies and gentlemen. I am Geneviéve Trabault the musical director for the quartet. Tonight our musicians wanted to open the concert with a movement from the familiar and well known Franz Schubert quintet in C major. Now, as you can see, we have only a quartet and Schubert wrote it as a quintet for two cellos. So right away we have a problem here. Excuse me for a moment..." she walked quickly to the wings, returning with a bow and cello. The audience broke into laughter spilling into hearty applause.

Madame Trabault continued: "I'll try to keep up with them. Then I'll get out of the way as the quartet plays, as you might expect, French composers. First, Debussy's lustrous string quartet in G minor—the fourth movement *tres modéré,* and end our concert with the striking finale of Ravel's quartet in F major.

Kathleen could not take her eyes off Pepe. How elegant he looked, she thought, in his black formal wear, his olive-skinned complexion in sharp contrast to the brilliant white of his shirt. She wondered if perhaps it was the stage lighting for he looked strikingly handsome.

She watched as Pepe's eyes searched the audience. It was doubtful that he could see beyond the first few rows. What was he looking for? Her? His gaze swept by her then, quickly returned and their eyes met. His mouth widened in an almost imperceptible expression of recognition. A blush found her. House lights dimmed. The concert began.

It was soon apparent that Madame Trabault was a very accomplished cellist, but Pepe played with equal passion and intensity. Throughout the Schubert selection they played off each other, neither yielding to the other. Kathleen was fascinated.

Then the quarter took up the Debussy and Ravel. Fifty-four minutes later they put down their bows to hearty applause punctuated by shouts of bravo. The audience demanded an encore and the quartet was prepared to give them one. Madame Trabault came back on stage for the obligatory acknowledgement of sponsorships and a few comments about the importance of this cultural exchange. The encore was a set of sprightly French folk melodies which was enthusiastically received by the audience.

Flushed with their performance the musicians packed up their cases for the trip back to the hotel. Madame Trabault gathered the group together: "You were fantastic out there! I'm so proud of you. You are great representatives of our country. Now, I have a few announcements. After we get back to the hotel and you have a chance to change clothes, Kathleen would like to buy us a round of drinks down stairs in the bar. The next two days we are on our own. Several of you have expressed interest in seeing a Broadway show. Let me know and I will try to get tickets. Lastly, I have to tell you that Pepe will be leaving us and returning early. He didn't want you to know until after the performance. Pepe…"

"I didn't want anything to distract from our concert. I have to go back. My grandmother is quite ill. She is eighty-eight, but she has always been in good health. I'm not exactly sure what the problem is. We are a very close family and I must go back. I'm sorry. I'll really miss seeing New York with you".

Paulette and Henri were quick to say they were sad to see him leave and wished him well. Margaux tried to hide her disappointment, then, gushed with concern for him. Kathleen held back.

She was both confused and disheartened, Kathleen. Why had Pepe not told her? Certainly he must feel he could confide in her. Maybe he had not had the opportunity…

Back at the hotel she found an unoccupied corner in the bar and began moving tables and chairs together. A waiter headed her way. The French would soon be down but she would not wait to order a drink.

"Are you Kathleen?" he asked.

"Yes," she said hesitantly.

"I thought as much. You fit the description. I have a message for you," he said, handing her a little envelope. "Can I get you something? A drink perhaps…?"

"I'm expecting five other people but I'll have a whisky sour while I'm waiting. Thank you."

She opened the envelope. On a card inside was neatly written:

> *Mon Cher* **Kathleen,**
> <u>**Must see you**</u>**. Can you meet me tomorrow in the lobby of** <u>**your**</u> **hotel at 8:00 a.m.?**
> *Avec Affection*,
> **Pepe**

Kathleen looked up as Madame Trabault and Paulette entered the room. The note was quickly tucked into her purse.

Paulette gave Kathleen a small gift of lavender-scented toiletries from Provence, along with her address and phone number. "If you have time," she said, "when you are in Nice for the concert give me a call. I could drive down and we could get together for a drink. I live not far from the city."

Within a few minutes Henri, Pepe and Margaux arrived. Everyone was in high spirits and casually dressed—most in sweaters and jeans. As the evening wore on they became louder, even boisterous, earning a few stares of disapproval from nearby tables. At one point Kathleen caught Pepe's eye, nodded slightly before looking away.

It was well after midnight when, for the last time, they thanked Kathleen, and returned to their rooms.

The phone jangled at Kathleen's bedside jerking her awake. "Good morning. The time is seven-fifteen," said the recorded voice.

She waited for him in the lobby, strolling nervously about. A few minutes after eight, he entered. He stopped, luggage in both hands, looking anxiously around. Then a grin widened his face when he saw her. She led him to the quiet alcove she had found the morning before. They sat, partially obscured by the greenery of the potted plant. Knees nearly touching, they looked at each other…she, searching, he, tense and vulnerable.

"I'm sorry and very disappointed that you have to go back to France," she said, "but if your grandmother is ill—"

"My Grandmother is a tough old bird. I wouldn't be surprised if she lived to be a hundred. There is another reason that I must return. It seems my father is concerned for my safety. The attack last night may not have accidental. It wasn't a robbery and they only seemed to want to hurt me…and not seriously at that."

Concern creased Kathleen's brow.

"You needn't be afraid. It's not about you. It's about me…and my family." He closed his eyes, struggling for words.

She took his hand in hers

"This…is crazy," he said shaking his head. "Absolutely crazy! I've known you for less than two days and I can't get you out of my mind. It isn't just infatuation, it's something more. I don't know what it is…" his voice trailed off.

She wanted to hold him. She moved closer.

"Crazy. I don't even know you, and you don't know me, but I was hoping in the next few days—"

"I'm coming to France in April, Kathleen offered. "I could see you then. But now, tell me more. About you, I mean. Why are you threatened?

He pulled back his sleeve. "I have to leave for the airport in twenty minutes. I'll tell you what I can. My father owns a company that has been quite successful. We are not extraordinarily wealthy but he has done well. He doesn't want to run the business anymore and wants to retire. The problem is, one of his competitors wants him to turn the business over to him and my father refuses to do so. But this man is determined to have it and he has a reputation of being unscrupulous, perhaps even dangerous. He has made threats that have made my father concerned and angry. My father doesn't feel I am safe here and feels I should come home until this is resolved."

Kathleen bit her lower lip thoughtfully. "Does this have something to do with the guys that attacked us on the street?"

"I don't know. He seems to think so—that it may have been intended as a warning."

"Here, in America?"

"It could have been meant to show how far this man's reach and influence can extend." Pepe could see fear in her eyes. "Actually," he added, "I'm fairly sure what happened on the street was unrelated, but of course it's possible that my father knows things I don't."

"Pepe, are you French?"

He laughed. "It's true, isn't it? I am the only one in my group who doesn't have a French name. My name is Giuseppe Benedetti, but ever since I can remember I've been called Pepe. My father and my grandfather before him were born on the island of Corsica. It is far closer to the coast of Italy than France, but the island has been a part of France for over two hundred years. In many ways my family thinks of themselves as Italian, but we are all French born citizens. We moved to the mainland when I was a boy because my father's business required it, but we still maintain the family home on the island. Of course now I am away at school most of the year, but my family lives in the hills above Nice—a little town called Gattiéres. It's cooler up there, and windy much of the year."

He peered at his watch again. "Oh, I must go. The time has gone too fast."

They stood and he took her gently by the shoulders and kissed her, then held her in his arms.

"Kathleen, when you come in April…if you have the time…"

"…we will spend some time together," she added softly. "My father is coming over for the concert. We were already planning to stay some extra days. Maybe I can add a few more."

Still with a perceptible limp he walked with her to the line of taxis waiting patiently outside. Halfway across the lobby he felt a tug at his coat.

"Please," she said, "just a second…"

He turned to see a little camera covering her face and a sharp blink of light.

"Now I have something to remember you by," she said.

They laughed. "Good," he said. "I want you to remember me."

As the cab pulled off, Kathleen thought of when, two nights ago at his hotel she had left *him* standing there. Now, it was as if part of her was leaving again—with him.

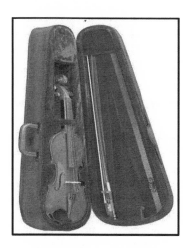

Chapter Eight

Grudgingly winter was releasing its hold and the days were becoming warmer and longer. It's mid-march, and Amherst College is only a week away from spring break.

Kathleen finished her last class of the week and with her backpack and violin case started to leave the music building. She was contemplating the weekend. She must stop at the grocery on the way back to her apartment, for her father was coming up tomorrow. She always looked forward to his occasional visits. Usually he would take her to some comfortable restaurant for dinner, but she had insisted that she would make diner herself. He relented when she enticed him with the promise of shepherd's pie—a favorite of his. It would be a quiet evening together, where father and daughter could catch up on each other's lives.

She was almost half way down the hall and nearly upon him when she saw him. He was standing against the wall, looking in her direction. Despite holding a violin case, he appeared strangely out of place in his pin-striped suit and tie. He was middle-aged with receding black hair combed straight back.

She was about to pass him when he stepped abruptly in her path.

"Miss Campbell...Kathleen Campbell?"

She hesitated, poised to more on. "Yes..."

"If you please, I would like to have a word with you," he said with a pronounced French accent. He saw the wariness in her eyes, and quickly added "I have a message from Pepe."

Surprised, she stood mouth agape.

He spoke again. "Is there some place we can talk for a few minutes?"

Gathering her senses as best she could, she led him to the coffee shop in the Campus Center building. It would be safe there.

Students and faculty milled about. They found a table and the man dutifully bought them coffee. In an attempt to put her somewhat at ease, he smiled. "Now then, Miss Campbell, I am here on behalf of Mr.

Benedetti—Pepe's father. He has sent me to thank you for coming to the aid of his son when he was attacked in the street."

"Really, I didn't do much. It happened so fast."

"Pepe told us what you did. Nevertheless your presence probably lessened the severity of the assault."

"Is he all right…Pepe, I mean?"

"He's fine. In fact I have a letter he wanted me to give you."

Kathleen's heart leaped…then she lowered her eyebrows. "You haven't come all this way to deliver a letter. One that could have easily been mailed—"

"That's true. I haven't. First there is something you must understand. It is a Corsican tradition that whenever a favor is given or a kindness is shown that it is always acknowledged in turn. Of course the same is true when someone has been wronged. I'm sure you know our word for it—*vendetta*.

Kathleen's fingers ran nervously along the rim of the table.

He placed the violin case on his knees and snapped open the top. "Mr. Benedetti would like you to have this. Pepe played this when he was a boy. Eventually he decided he wanted to play a larger stringed instrument and switched to the cello. This violin is quite old. Although I personally wouldn't know, I'm told it has an exceptional sound."

Nestled in the velvet lined case, the little violin had a lustrous soft-textured finish with rich orange/brown hues. Kathleen brushed it with her fingertips. It appeared to be in good condition despite its age, but had obviously seen considerable use.

"Oh, I couldn't possibly accept this," she said, overwhelmed by the generosity of it.

The man slowly shook his head. "That is not possible. No, Miss Campbell, you must. Such a gift cannot be refused. It would be impolite to the point of being a rejection of Mr. Benedetti's generosity. He wants that you should have it."

She hesitated. "Very well, then. Please tell Mr. Benedetti that I am very touched by his gift and his thoughtfulness. I will cherish this violin."

He snapped the case shut and placed it on the table between them.

"One more thing you should know," he said. "This cannot be an actual gift to you. It is much too valuable to be given and accepted as a gift, as you would be obliged to pay gift taxes and they would be substantial. This is thought to have been made in Cremona, Italy by Giuseppe Guarneri and has been authenticated by two reputable dealers. One of those experts gave a qualified opinion only because it is slightly smaller than any other known Guarneri violin."

He reached in his breast pocket, smiling slyly. "You should consider this violin on loan to you from Mr. Benedetti—a permanent loan." He withdrew a small envelope and handed it to Kathleen. On it was simply written: "*Kathleen*". "Pepe wanted me to give you this. Now if you will excuse me I think I have finished my business here."

He rose, putting his hand on the violin case. "Take good care of it," he said. He walked briskly away and soon disappeared among the students crowding the corridors of the student center.

Kathleen sat in a daze. She hadn't touched her coffee. She took a sip, then pushed it aside and tore open the envelope.

Mon Cher Kathleen,

I hope you accept this gift from my father. It was his idea, and an attempt to thank you for "protecting" his only son. It is his way. I hope you are not offended.

I am very familiar with this violin, having played it when I was younger. It has been in the family for a long time, although I don't know how we came by it.

It may appear a little delicate but I assure you it's not. You can dig into it with your bow and it will respond with full rich tones.

I miss you greatly and look forward to your concert here. Sometime after the concert would it be possible for me to show you around Provence? If possible, I would like to take you to Gattiéries and have you meet my family.

I suppose you are in rehearsal, or soon will be. I can't wait to hear you play!

Avec Amour et Affection,
Pepe

She lifted the letter to her lips then returned it to its envelope. Slinging her backpack over her shoulder and gathering a violin case in each hand she headed for the parking lot. Her head was swimming. She must not forget to stop at the grocery. She had promised her father shepherd's pie. She had so much to tell him!

†

They were nearly through dinner when Kendall Campbell leaned back in his chair. He dabbed at the corner of his mouth with his napkin and vigorously nodded his head. "This is just excellent, Kathleen. As they say, just like my mother used to make. Your mother tried to make it once or twice but never could quite manage it."

He leaned forward again, chasing errant remnants around his plate with his fork. "Now," he said without looking up, "when are you going to tell me what's on your mind?"

Kathleen smiled innocently. "Whatever do you mean?" she teased.

"My dear, I know you better than anyone else in the world. You have something you've waiting to tell me."

"Can you wait for dessert?"

"Just as long as you don't forget to serve it..."

"Good. Go sit in your chair and I'll get you a glass of port."

He always enjoyed a glass after dinner. Port, not sherry. The overstuffed chair was the only one of its kind in her spartan apartment. He sank into it with a satisfied moan and she brought him his port in her only crystal glass.

"Now, what's this all about?" he said expectantly.

She pulled up a chair and told her story. Kendall listened intently but said nothing. Brow furrowed, he sipped his wine. Everything spilled out—and when she told it she felt better for it.

Finally, she disappeared into her bedroom, returning with the violin and placed it on his knees. Without a word he took it from its case and for several minutes the professor turned it about in his hands, examing it in great detail. His fingertips followed the contour of the purfling, caressing the head, the ʃ-holes and the texture of the finish. No bit of wear or blemish went unnoticed. It was quiet, except for the wail of a distant siren and the barking of a neighborhood dog.

Then he spoke. "I'm really not experienced in this area. Most of what I know in art history is in the visual arts. Antiquities and something like this…" his voice trailed off.

But Kathleen was anticipating his response and he knew it.

"Very few of these violins are authentic," he began. 'This does look quite old but I doubt it's a Guarneri or one of the other Italian masters. If it was a Guarneri it could be worth millions, even in poor condition. Why would this Benedetti fellow give away such a priceless object? It doesn't make sense. Even with my limited expertise I can see it is not a Guarneri. The detail is too precise. The craftsmanship is much too fine. Have you played it?"

"I have. It's not easy to play. It is demanding of the violinist. Here, let me tune it and play for you." She took it back into the bedroom.

Kendall sat, pondering what he had seen and heard. A father was supposed to have answers, solutions. But it isn't always so, and he didn't have any here. He heard her tuning and wrestled with all she had told him. Who was this man that had sent an emissary three thousand miles to deliver an expensive if not priceless violin? What was his motive? His son's interest in his daughter, perhaps? Was the incident on the sidewalk in New York somehow more sinister than it appeared?

Kathleen reentered with two violins and a bow. "First, I'll play my violin. Then I'll play the other. See what you think."

When she finished she put down her bow and looked expectantly at her father.

"Kathleen, they were both very nice, but the old one had a different sound. Very distinctive. Full, more powerful. But I am not a trained musician and that is all I can tell you."

"In your own way you have told me what I thought myself," she said sitting beside him. "What do you make of it all?"

"Under the circumstances I don't know how you could not have accepted this gift. You could hardly have done otherwise. Do you know the name of Benedetti's company? Have a card perhaps, his address?"

"Only that the family lives in Gattiéres, somewhere in the hills above Nice."

"That's not much. I'll go on the internet and see if I can find out, although I don't know what I should be looking for or what to expect—if anything. Anyway, I'm glad I'm going over to your concert."

"Are you ready for dessert?" She busied herself in the little alcove she called her kitchen.

"You know I have to ask," said Kendall. "How much do you like this guy/"

"Pepe…? I like him a lot more than I have reason to—considering how little time I've known him. I trust him, if that's what you mean."

"That's part of what I mean," he said simply.

ROBERT MITCHELL

Chapter Nine

She peered anxiously out the window as the plane made its final approach into Nice. The overnight flight from New York to Paris had been long and tedious and Kathleen had only been able to doze-off from time to time. Now, on the last leg of her journey the morning was clear and sunny. It was a perfect day to fly into Nice, for when clear the view was spectacular. The pilots had invited the only flight attendant on board into the cockpit for a birds-eye view, and passengers were craning their necks to see the landscape below. As usual the winds off the Mediterranean swept over the hills above the city and the plane tossed in the air currents.   Kathleen watched as the deep blue-green of the sea came into view, quickly followed by the long crescent of the harbor with the city of Nice nestled tightly along it.

Beside her and across the aisle were the other members of her quartet. Lin Liu, a petite Chinese-American woman was the other violinist and Annie Henriksen, tall and blond, played the cello. A tall, lanky young man with an unruly mop of red hair was the violist, Tom Fitzgerald. Their music director did not accompany them. The quartet was well rehearsed and prepared for their concert and he saw little purpose in his presence at the performance.

At the airport a row of taxi drivers waited impatiently for their passengers. The trunks of the first two cabs in line flew open in anticipation of the four musicians struggling with their baggage and instrument cases.

Kathleen handed the driver her bag but kept the violin case to herself. "Do you speak English?" she asked.

"*Oui, oui!*" Then, with a heavy accent asked "Where are you going?"

"The Hotel Beau Rivage. You know it?"

"But of course," he replied tapping his head with his fingers. "The Beau Rivage had already been a hotel here for a hundred years before I was even born."

The taxi ahead of them sped off with Annie and Tom. Lin and Kathleen no sooner slid onto the well-worn seat than the driver slammed the door. With no perceptive concern for traffic he swung away from the curb.

"Many famous people have stayed at the hotel. Of course that was before it was renovated a few years ago. Personally, I liked it the way it was. They redid it in a modern theme, and of course their prices went up as well. That is the way with our city…the very old inevitably yields to the new," he said with a sigh.

He paused to swing abruptly into another lane. A horn sounded behind them. "This is our main street that runs four miles along the beach—the *Promenade des Anglais*." He cut across traffic and up a side street. "The part of Nice that has changed the least is the Old Port. There are many eighteenth century buildings with shutters and red exteriors. I live in one."

The driver pulled in behind the other taxi and lurched to a stop in front of the Beau Rivage. Festooned with flags, the old building had a street level façade of marble slabs set into a contemporary design.

The Americans had been told that their French host would meet them at the hotel. In fact, she had been waiting for them. Kathleen did not see her until she heard the voice behind her.

"Kathleen, how good to see you!"

She turned to face Margaux. After the initial surprise, Kathleen fumbled with a greeting and introduced her three companions.

"Unfortunately,' said Margaux "check-in time is not until two o'clock. You will have to check your bags until then."

Not wanting to leave their violins in the storage room Kathleen and Lin Lui had the hotel secure them in their vault. It did not go unnoticed by Margaux.

"We have three hours to kill", said Margaux. "This hotel is on the rue Saint Francois de Paule. It is a very interesting street. A cross from us and down the street is the Nice Opera House. It is old and quite grand, with three tiers of box seats surrounding the stage. It's closed now, but I have arranged for us to have a look inside. Across the street from the Opera House is where you will play your concert—the Church of Saint Francois de Paule, built in the eighteen century in the Baroque and neoclassical style of the times. Farther down the street is the outdoor market which will be closing up about now. There are many good restaurants along the way where we can stop for lunch."

They sat outside for lunch, an umbrella providing a circle of shade. For the first time, Kathleen was aware that she had been studying Margaux. In New York she had thought her introspective and a bit sullen. Now, she seemed pleasant enough, outgoing and comfortable in her role as host.

Still there was something deeper. She appeared to be one of those people who play the role of someone other than who they are...another person behind who you saw. Kathleen's father had always told her she "wore her heart on her sleeve", and she did not relate well to someone like Margaux. Perhaps, she thought, Margaux sensed something between her and Pepe. Yes...maybe that was it—a trace of jealousy. Whatever it was it made Kathleen uneasy.

✝

A heady scent filled her hotel room before Kathleen even saw them. A large bouquet of spring flowers spilled over their vase. She immediately opened the card.

Welcome to Provence!
I expect to be at your concert.
Can't wait to see you. Will contact you later.

Pepe

She thought she thought of calling her father but it would still be night in Boston. Instead she punched in a text message: *arrived ok. checked in. hotel holding rm 4 u. nice place! k*

Kathleen was exhausted but it was only late afternoon. Too early to sleep... She would just lay down for a few minutes. The room was dark when she awoke.

ROBERT MITCHELL

Chapter Ten

It was mid-afternoon on Sunday. The seats in Saint Francois de Paule Church were nearly filled. Heads looked up from their programs and applause broke out as the Americans entered carrying their instruments. Speaking in French, Margaux introduced the quartet and made some program comments.

Kathleen looked out over the audience, a proud father conspicuous in the first row. She could not find Pepe in the crowd. She wondered if he had come.

He had. Sitting in the back of the church Pepe peered through opera glasses. Framed within the circle was Kathleen. In her hand was her regular violin, not the old one given as a gift. Good, he thought. It was safer that way.

The concert's repertoire was selections from Dvorak's American Quartet, Brahms, a piece by Edward Elgar—and an encore of pop music, including "Let's Fall in Love", "Crazy for You" and "Come Away with Me".

The audience was genuinely enthusiastic and the American quartet flushed with pride and accomplishment.

The quartet began packing their instruments and sheet music, stopping occasionally as audience members approached to express their appreciation. Meanwhile, in the lobby of the Beau Rivage two men waited for the quartet's return.

Kendall Campbell and Pepe Benedetti cast casual glances at each other. Finally, Kendall strolled to where Pepe was sitting.

"Excuse me. Are you by chance Pepe?"

"Oui, oh…yes! And you…Professor Campbell, perhaps?"

They laughed at the irony of their meeting.

"Apparently my daughter's descriptions of us are fairly accurate," said Kendall. "Kathleen has told me about you."

"Not unpleasantly, I hope."

"On the contrary, she has spoken...highly of you."

"You must be very proud of your daughter. It was a very impressive concert, and I had not heard her play before today. She is very talented."

"She is very serious about her music. It's a big part of her life."

Pepe paused..."When they return I am planning to invite everyone to a post-concert reception. I hope you'll join us."

"But I'm not part of the quartet; I would be awkward—out of place."

"No, I insist! You must come. I was planning on you being there...but you have other plans —"

"I don't have any plans as I thought Kathleen would want to be with her friends tonight. Are you sure you want all six of us?"

"Six?"

"The quartet, Margaux and me."

"Oh, Margaux won't be coming'" he said uncomfortably, searching for the proper words. "You see Margaux's family and mine don't get along very well. I'm afraid it's a longstanding and difficult situation. Very unfortunate. Margaux knows she cannot accept an invitation to where she is not welcome Nevertheless, we are casual acquaintances.." He hesitated. "Actually you must be careful around Margaux. I'm not sure she can be trusted."

Ann Henriksen suddenly appeared, wrestling her cello case through the glass doors of the hotel, assisted by Margaux and the other three musicians. They immediately spotted Pepe and hurried over. Kathleen, taken by surprise to see her father and Pepe together, joined them.

A hearty round of greetings and introductions followed. Kathleen's heart pounded with the excitement of it all. Here, at last, was Pepe, looking every bit as handsome and gallant as she remembered.

"I'm here," announced Pepe scanning the group "to invite you all to a reception in recognition of your concert here in France. I would like to show you some of Provence as we drive up into the hills where I live. There we will have dinner. I think you will find it interesting. For those of you who may have other plans…I certainly understand."

All accepted enthusiastically, except Margaux, who, unfortunately had other plans. Excited with the prospect of the evening ahead, they agreed to meet in the lobby in an hour.

Although Pepe had assured them it would be a casual affair, the three women decided to "dress up". Tom had little choice but to go along with it. Kathleen, anxious and excited, especially wanted to make a good impression on Pepe and his parents. She slipped into a black knee length dress. She added a string of pearls, hesitated…then grabbed a pair of shoes which as an after- thought had brought along. Quite high heeled and bordering on stilettos, she had bought them once on impulse. They were "unlike her" she thought and had never worn them. Tonight she would. The rest of her wardrobe was conservative—this would add some flair.

She had a few minutes before meeting the group in the lobby so she called Paulette, the French exchange student, who had suggested that she call when in Nice. They agreed to meet for lunch in the days after the concert. Near the end of the conversation Kathleen mentioned that Pepe had invited the Americans to his home for the evening. There was a pause, then Paulette asked: "How well do you know Pepe?"

"Not well," Kathleen replied.
"I like Pepe, but he does have *bagages*...some baggage. But then, I guess we all do—"

The conversation ended shortly thereafter and the curious comment was largely forgotten.

A black limousine with tinted windows wove its way along the coastline of the city. Inside, Pepe pointed out historical sights and other points of interest.

"The fort you see on the hill at the end of the beach was built in the seventeenth century to protect the city. It's closed inside now, but the climb up there gives a great view of the city. Now— if you look out in the harbor you will see steel beams in the form of crosses that the Germans sunk off shore as a defense to an Allied invasion that never came here. They are still here almost seventy years later."

He said a few words to the driver and they swung off into the hills above Nice. The road wove past gated homes interrupted by little clusters of picturesque shops.

Pepe turned to face the group. "I have an admission to make. Tonight is not just a reception for you. We will be joining others who my parents have invited this evening. When I suggested you might like to come they insisted that I invite you. That's why this happened so spontaneously. I'm sorry for that, but I'm just glad you could come tonight. I think you will enjoy yourselves. The entertainment is a well-known singer—especially here in Provence. We will also try to see that you get some good French food." He threw up his hands, "*Viola!* What more can I say…"

He was charming in a boyish sort of way, Kathleen thought. Sitting next to him in the limousine she moved a bit closer. The car wound up the steep road that snaked up from the sea slowing, somewhat, for hairpin turns. Up they climbed, past a mixture of palm trees and other tropical vegetation interspersed with conifers of cypress and juniper. It seemed strangely incongruous to the Americans.

In about twenty minutes they entered Gattiéres, an ancient village with roads to match. They passed flower laden village squares with archaic drinking fountains. Past charming old houses and passageways with restored facades and doorways. At a small roundabout in the center of the village the driver pulled sharply onto a road barely wide enough for two cars.

On the outskirts of the village they pulled up to the gate of a large villa set back some distance down a driveway lined with stately plane and sycamore trees. A young man, watering some shrubs, watched them as the limousine turned up the drive. Near the house another man with a wheelbarrow of dead palm fronds stood frozen, staring intently. Parked off to the side of the stone villa were half a dozen cars.

As if in anticipation of their arrival, Pepe's father and mother greeted them at the door. Kathleen studied them nervously. They were not anything like she had imagined.

Anthony Benedetti, older than she expected, was a grandfatherly man with receding gray hair combed straight back. Handsome and fit for his age, his face was nonetheless creased from time. He was simply but impeccably dressed in a striped freshly pressed dress shirt and Italian designer slip-on shoes.

"I'm Pepe's father," he said not waiting for an introduction. His voice was soft—smooth as velvet, a man obviously used to being listened to without raising his voice. "I am Anthony Benedetti, but we are not formal here. Please call me Tony. We all speak English—if not well, adequately. We will practice it on you."

He appeared both self-assured and gracious, traits that often do not fit well together.

I'm not in charge here," he continued. "That would be Pepe's grandmother who you will meet later. Next comes my wife—Pepe's mother, Maria. I come in somewhere after that."

"He exaggerates! Don't listen to him," interrupted Maria. She was noticeably younger than her husband. Her hair, coal black, was drawn back and held in place with tortoise shell picks. This accentuated a long slender neck, giving her an aristocratic appearance. She had managed to retain much of her youthful figure and she was, by all measure, a striking and attractive woman.

"In about an hour the rest of our guests will be arriving," she said, "a few friends, but mostly officials and businessmen from the area. You may find them interesting," she rolled her eyes "some more than others. But tonight, consider yourselves our special guests. I'm so glad you've come. You'll add some spontaneity and liveliness to the evening. We're going to have some drinks and food—also some good music, so please enjoy your selves."

At this point a woman whispered in Maria's ear. "If you will excuse me now—I'm told the musicians are here and want to know where to set up."

Anthony Benedetti took Kendall Campbell by the arm for a stroll around the grounds.

Pepe herded the others out to a large terrace overlooking the Var valley far below. The view from the terrace was spectacular. Drinks were served and everyone soon settled into padded deck chairs scattered about. Shortly, Pepe's mother came out and said a few words to him in Italian. He nodded and drew Kathleen aside.

"Come inside with me," he said. "Grandmother wishes to see you."

Kathleen recoiled with uncertainty. Why would the old woman want to see her?

"It's all right," he assured her. "Of course I've told her about you. She is the matriarch of the family and we give her the respect she deserves. Grandmother is ninety-two. She is frail, but has lost none of her mind. She is sharp and uncannily perceptive. I think you'll like her. Do you mind?"

"No…I think I'd like to meet her."

The door opened into a large room. A wheelchair faced the flickering flames of a fireplace. The room was warm almost stifling. Pepe and Kathleen stood in the doorway.

"Grandmother…?"

The figure stirred and wheeled around to face them. Pepe took Kathleen by the arm and led her to the old woman.

"Grandmother, this is Kathleen, the woman I told you about—the woman in New York."

"Thank you for coming upstairs to see me," she said in near perfect English. She motioned to a chair nearby. "Please sit, my dear. Pepe, if you don't mind…" she said gesturing with a long boney finger towards the door," Kathleen and I would like a moment together."

He hesitated, then "I'll be right back, Kathleen."

Grandmother sat with a little blanket on her lap. Her white wispy hair was pulled back in the same style as her daughter-in-law Maria. The translucence of her hands and face was mottled by nearly a century under the Mediterranean sun.

"Living as long as I have is both a blessing and a curse, Kathleen. It's a blessing when I see someone like you with such beauty and vitality."

A blush colored Kathleen's face. She was at a loss how to respond.

"It's all right, my dear," said the grandmother "enjoy it while you can. I understand you've been given the violin. Is it in a safe place?"

"It's secure in my apartment in America. I thought of bringing it here, but I need more time to really be comfortable with it. I love its sound and in time will become the one I play."

"Good. A violin needs to be played to maintain its capability. This violin has a sad history. It was seized from its Jewish owner in Austria during the war by a collector. I don't think it was ever played again until it my husband acquired it and Pepe began playing it. He was a very young boy then. I remember his music teacher thought the sound would come back, and it did. One can only imagine how it must have sounded when it was made! Anyway, it's really just an old wooden box. Its true value is in the sound it can still make. I'm glad you have it now."

"I'm very grateful to have it."

"Now tell me. What is your interest in my grandson?"

"Well...I like him very much. Of course I don't know him well, but he seems gentle and kind. Somehow I feel safe with him. He is also quite good looking—it must run in the family."

A twinkle appeared in the old woman's watery blue eyes and a smile twitched at her mouth. "It does! You are quite perceptive. All of the things you've said about Pepe are true. However you must keep in mind that you are from very different worlds. Sometimes things in life can't be what we would like them to be, but rather only what they are. Still...love can be expressed in many ways."

Kathleen was struggling to find the meaning in the grandmother's words when Pepe entered.

"I hope you two are about finished," he said. "There's a party going on downstairs! Are you coming down grandmother?"

"In time. Go now, Kathleen. You've been very kind to talk to me."

Kathleen took the gnarled hand in hers. "I'm so glad to meet you and to have had this little talk. Thank you...grandmother."

"Bless you, my dear. Now you two go. I'll be down later. The evening wouldn't be complete without that horrid mayor telling me all the things he has done for the village. I can't stand that man. Unfortunately there will be others like him. You'd better have someone send me up a glass of sherry. Boors...absolute boors..." she mumbled, turning her chair back to the fire.

With Kendall Campbell at his side, Anthony Benedetti pinched off the dead end of a vine clinging to the inside wall that surrounded the villa.

"Maria and I have lived here for thirty-six years. We spend most of the year here. We are three hundred meters above the sea so it is much cooler than down on the coast. In November we go back to Corsica until spring. I was born on the island and we still have the old family home on the northwest coast."

They strolled a few steps in silence.

"Pepe tells me you're a professor in Boston?"

"I'm not a full professor, actually. At least not yet. I teach art history at a college in Boston."

Benedetti's eyebrows rose. "You are an expert then in old art and antiquities?"

"Well that's my area. An expert—" he waggled his hand.

"I've had the opportunity to collect a few things. I really can't say I'm a collector. I've never searched them out, but if they came my way—"

"Really! I would like to see them."

"Oh, I'm afraid we don't have much on display, although you may see a few vases and small sculptures around the house tonight."

They had walked full circle around the grounds and were back at the steps leading to the terrace.

"Let's go up Kendall. I'll make you a drink. Then I suppose I should greet the guests. Make yourself at home."

Kendall joined the youthful Americans on the terrace while Benedetti hurried off to play the host.

Perhaps assisted by liquor, as the evening wore on conversation flowed easily and many French guests stopped to engage the Americans. An extravagant buffet was set out followed by wandering kitchen help with silver trays of tempting petit fours.

Grandmother made her appearance amid clamorous guests vying for her attention. Through the crowd Kathleen caught glimpses of her with her thin lips fixed in a brave, tolerant little smile. She actually caught her eye once and gave the old woman a cheerful thumbs-up. Grandmother smile broadened and nodded back. At one point Kendall Campbell was taken by Maria to meet old woman and they exchanged a few words.

Then—a drum roll and a rim shot from the band. As if on command people began taking their seats, respectfully leaving the front row for their hosts. Maria snatched Kendall and escorted him to a seat beside her. Pepe was quick to do the same with Kathleen, while motioning the rest of the quartet to seats in the front. Grandmother, of course, sat center front.

Anthony Benedetti stood expectantly in front of the five piece orchestra, microphone in hand. Finally the seats were filled.

"Thank you all for joining us for what I think is going to be a great evening of entertainment. Maria and I have known this performer since early in her career. Now she has become one of the most exciting and popular singers in the south of France. Her singing style has been described as a mixture of Marlene Dietrich with a dash of Ute Lemper and Edith Piaf. Here is our dear friend and an incredible talent…Abrielle Benoit!"

Kathleen was impressed by how glib and comfortable Pepe's father was before a crowd. Moreover, apparently out of respect for the Americans, he had spoken in English. It was too good. He must have rehearsed it, she thought. She realized she liked this family, and it was different from any she had known.

The singer entered in a satin burgundy-colored evening gown and she sang for half an hour, working the little audience with all the drama and intensity that only French singers can seem to wring from a song. She sang the old favorites, effortlessly easing between French and English. *"Let's Call It A Day", La vie en rose", "Time On My Hands", "Illusions"* and ending the evening with a beautiful arrangement of *"Falling in Love Again".* Intentionally or not, she sang several lines directly to Kathleen and Pepe;

> *"Falling in love again,*
> *Never wanted to.*
> *What can I say?*
> *I can't help it."*

While she was singing Pepe put his arm around Kathleen, neither caring who saw it. She was entranced—a bit light headed from the drinks no doubt.

Meanwhile, her father, seated by Maria, was beginning to feel uncomfortable. In the ambiance of the evening, and wanting to be a hospitable guest, he had not declined many drinks offered him…and he was feeling it. He was overdue in finding a bathroom. Excusing himself, he wandered about until in desperation he asked one of the serving help.

"Excuse me, where is there a bathroom?"

She looked at him inquiringly. *"Qu'avez-vous dit?"*

"Toilet—the toilets, *s'il vous plait?"*

"Ah—"she said in a burst of understanding *"toilettes!"* She led the way—but the door was closed. It was occupied. She hesitated, then motioned him to follow her to the bottom of a large spiral staircase. Pointing up the stairs she then vigorously motioned to the right.

He nodded. "*Merci, madame*". When he got to the top of the stairs every door on the corridor was closed. Kendall turned to his right. Not surprisingly every door looked the same. Finally he found himself facing a door at the end of the hall. Slowly he turned the door handle and peered in. It was dark. His fingers brushed along the wall searching for a light switch. He found it.

It was not a bathroom, but a large office or study. Across the room a substantial desk faced the door. He was about to leave when suddenly he realized what he had seen. Blinking in disbelief he drew in a little breath. On the wall behind the desk hung an oil painting—not large, little more than two feet wide, a little less tall and mounted in a gilded gold frame.

Kendall recognized it immediately. He had seen it before, hanging in the Gardner Museum in Boston. "The Concert" by Johannes Vermeer had been stolen, along with others, from the museum more than a decade ago. They had never been recovered.

He shouldn't stay, and reached to turn off the light. Maybe it was the drinks, or perhaps the intrigue of the moment—it didn't matter, for against his better judgment he had to have a closer look.

The painting was of a young woman playing the harpsichord, a gentleman listening. Typical of this painter, pictures hung on the walls—pictures within the picture— and rectangular black and white floor tiles. As customary for Jan Vermeer, light came through an unseen window on the left side.

Kendall examined the edges of the painting. The thieves had cut it from its frame, and now reframed it would be missing a fraction of an inch on each side. Also, the museum had maintained a thick file describing and noting every detail and characteristic of this mid-seventeenth century masterpiece. Information in this dossier could fairly easily determine the authenticity of the original from a forgery.

Standing directly in front of the painting he shook his head in an attempt to clear his mind. He was not intoxicated but he clearly had enough drinks to feel somewhat light headed and unsteady. As best he could, Kendall studied the brush strokes, the opalescence of the woman's skirt—the folds soft and delicate. There was no signature. Vermeer seldom signed his work.

Downstairs a peal of laughter from the guests found its way up the staircase and into the room jarring Kendall from his concentration. Realizing how precarious his situation he hurried out of the room, closing the door after him. The hallway was empty and no one was in sight until he reached the top of the staircase. He slipped back into the party, winding his way through the crowd to the bathroom. Mercifully, this time it was unoccupied.

Chapter Ten

Ten o'clock. Still relatively early in the evening, especially by French standards, but some of the guests were beginning to depart. Perhaps not surprisingly considering the little soirée had started early—and it *was* a Sunday night.

Kathleen found her father in casual conversation with a French couple who, as she approached, drifted on.

"Have you been having a good time?" she asked.

"I've had a great time. It's been a very interesting evening, believe me. I ran into the rest of our group a few minutes ago. I think we're all about ready to leave."

"I'll tell Pepe. I was looking for you to tell you I'm going to stay awhile longer. It's only a little after ten. Pepe will take me back to the hotel."

"Kathleen, I'm not sure that's a good idea."

"Don't worry. I only plan to stay for an hour or so. I want to spend more time with Pepe."

Kendall wrestled with his apprehensions, although he wasn't at all sure what they were. He had always been overprotective of his daughter and he knew it. But she was twenty-three now and living on her own. Of course there was the painting in the study. However, he couldn't think of any risk in her staying.

"The roads" he said, grasping "—the roads here are treacherous."

She hugged him reassuringly. "I'll be fine. You and the others go. I'll be back by midnight."

The limousine driver was summoned and, after profusely thanking the Benedetti's, Kendall and the three American students sank into the black leather seats for their ride down the hills to Nice.

It was a warm evening for this time of year. The moon was full. Only a few guests remained and for

Kathleen and Pepe the prospect of being alone was enticing.

"Let's go out on the terrace," he said. "We have so much to talk about—so much I want to say."

When they stepped outside four men were sitting at a table smoking. Several looked up as the couple entered. One, his mouth around a cigar, stared at Kathleen through a curl of smoke.

Pepe took her arm. "Let's go down and walk in the garden."

As they passed the men, by chance the one with the cigar reached out to an ashtray, carefully rolling the ashes off the end.

Kathleen gasped—pausing in mid-step. Without lifting his head the man's eyes shifted from the ashtray to Kathleen. Quickly regaining her composure she moved on.

"What a beautiful evening!" she said in a voice louder than necessary.

"Pepe said something in response but she didn't hear. Her mind was racing. He put his arm around her and he felt that she was tense and rigid. A stone bench appeared out of the shadows.

"Let's sit down," she said, pulling him down.

"Is something wrong?"

"I don't know. Maybe. Pepe, that man on the terrace —the one with the cigar, I've seen him before."

"You couldn't have."

"But I have! It's the oddest thing. When he reached for the ashtray I saw a tattoo around his wrist…then I recognized him. I saw him in New York the morning your quartet arrived."

Even in the light of the moon she could see Pepe stiffen. For a brief moment he said nothing, then, took her hand.

"You must tell me everything. Kathleen, this is very important." There was a sense of urgency in his voice.

"Well…I was waiting in the lobby of my hotel for the van to arrive—the one which was to take us to Lincoln Center. It was early so I found a quiet area off the lobby. Near me were two men. One was the man I saw tonight. The other wore a hoodie—a jacket with a hood. He looked like he could be Hispanic and they didn't look like two men who would be together so out of curiosity I watched them. I couldn't hear what they were saying, of course. Then this man gave the other something—some papers, an envelope maybe."

She shivered. He took off his coat jacket and put it around her.

"And when he reached out I saw a tattoo on his wrist. How many men have tattoos on their wrists? It was the same one as the man on the terrace. When I saw that tattoo tonight it all came back and I recognized his face."

"What exactly did the tattoo look like? Can you describe it?"

"It's hard to describe. Spears or pitchforks—interconnected,"

Pepe's jaw tightened. "How sure are you that this is the same man?"

Kathleen hesitated. She sensed that this was somehow very serious. "I'm positive. I recognized him…and I think he may have recognized *me*. Tell me! What's going on?"

"When he was young this man belonged to a Corsican gang. This is their symbol—the trident, the three pointed spear of the god of the sea. But it is also the symbol of the devil, and that's what they called themselves the *Diavolo Discepoli.*"

He looked around nervously. "Kathleen, this is not at all good," he said in a calm but earnest voice, not wanting to alarm her. "We may not have much time but I can tell you this. I'm not involved in the company itself and my father doesn't want me to be, but his import and export business has a competitor who is known to be very cunning and even ruthless. We have known for some time that there is someone inside my father's business that is giving this competitor inside information—a spy in the company. Thanks to you I know who it is. The man with the tattoo. His name is Fillipo. You and I are the only ones that know and that is dangerous. What you have told me makes sense now. I have to talk to my father right away. You'll have to go back to your hotel right away but I can't drive you, I'll get a man to take you back—René, you can trust him." He stopped short.

Then…"Have you ever fired a gun?"

"I used to go hunting with my father all the time."

"Have you ever had or used a handgun?"

"Well, we used to shoot one for target practice…why?"

I'm going to give you a little gun. It's small and will fit in your purse. I want you to take it, just for tonight. I'll come to the hotel tomorrow and pick it up."

"Oh, I can't."

" Why not?"

"I don't have a permit—I never got one."

He laughed. Somehow it broke the tension and Kathleen felt better for it.

"Don't worry, we don't have permits here." He thought it better not to tell her that owning or carrying a handgun was against the law in France.

"Pepe, If we're in that much danger shouldn't we call the police?"

"No!" he said firmly "there is a lot you don't understand. This competitor is a very dangerous man but the police will want proof. If we wait until he acts it will be too late. We have to take precautions now."

Still, Kathleen was reluctant. "Do I have to take the gun?"

"I think you should. Just to be safe. Now—we must go."

They stood and he held her close, her hair brushing his cheek. How safe and reassuring she felt in his arms!

"I love you, Kathleen," he whispered in her ear. They kissed and suddenly the chill of the night air fell away. They stood, embracing each other in the moonlight.

"We have to go now," he said softly.

"I know..." she murmured.

They hurried to the front of the villa. It was brightly lighted and clusters of guests, reluctant to end the evening, were gathered in animated conversation.

"Stay here by the door I'll be right back".

When he reappeared he moved close to Kathleen, his body shielding their movements from view. From his pocket he pulled a small pistol not much bigger than the palm of his hand.

"It's loaded, but it can't fire unless both the trigger and the back of the grip are depressed. It can't go off accidentally—you have to intentionally fire it. Here's the safety—this is on, this off. You've made me feel a lot better by taking it. I'll see you at the hotel in the morning after this all is sorted out. Now, let me find René. He'll take you back.

"She opened her purse and he slipped it in. A brief kiss and he was gone. She stood under the glare of the lights by the door watching the departing guests and the activity around her. Soon a car pulled up and the driver got out and waved her over. He opened the back door and stood waiting for her.

"René?" she asked.

He nodded and motioned for her to get in. *"Oui, madame."*

Anthony Benedetti stood behind his desk in the room at the far end of the upstairs hall. Pepe and two other men looked on grimly. He slammed his hand on the desk and his eyes narrowed.

"Fillipo! His father and I went to school together in Corsica. He begged me to give his son a job just to get him out of the gang there. "

Antonio's rage quickly transitioned into controlled anger. It was obviously time to get down to the business at hand.

"Pepe, how sure is she about the tattoo?"

"Positive. Fillipo was the man in New York. She recognized him when she saw the tattoo again tonight. Kathleen thought he may have recognized her as well."

Antonio looked at one of the men. "Check the records. See where he was on the twenty-fourth of January."

"I have," he said waving a sheath of papers. "From the twenty-second until the twenty-eighth he wasn't working or on call. He took time off to move an aunt in Marseilles into a nursing home. "

"Who does he seem to be close to here?"

"No one in particular," said the other man. "Either there is no one else or he has been very cautious not to attract attention to anyone."

Antonio shifted in his chair. "Put some men on him. I don't want him to leave." Oh, another thing...while I'm thinking of it you'd better get the art out of here for a while. Take out the Vermeer and the Cézanne "Boy in the Red Vest"—and any other sculptures or things that could be a problem."

Suddenly there was an urgent knock at the door. It quickly opened and a man stepped in, closing it after him.

It was René! "Pepe" he said breathlessly "I waited for Madame Campbell but she wasn't there. After a minute or so and she didn't appear I asked the other drivers. They said that Paulo had just picked her up—no more than two minutes before. Paulo's not one of our drivers!"

Instantly all energy drained from Pepe's body. He didn't breathe and weakly reached out to a wall for support.

"My God," he gasped "they've got Kathleen!"

His father looked down at his desk in silence. Finally he said quietly "They have quite a head start but send out some cars to look for them...then bring Fillipo down to the cellar."

Kathleen watched the lights of the little village of Gattieres disappear behind her. She was vaguely uneasy. René didn't appear to speak any English and her feeble attempts at French didn't solicit much of any response. And was it really necessary for the French to drive so fast? It was late Sunday evening and little traffic—but why such a race to get down?

Most of the inhabitants along the mountain road had gone to bed, their quaint homes and shops standing dark in the moonlight. The driver turned onto another road and there began to be fewer buildings and more open land. Pastures and orchards, carved out of the hillsides.

Fear crept inside her. Kathleen sensed something was terribly wrong.

"Where are we going? This is not the road," she shouted at the driver.

"C"est OK! C'est OK!" he yelled back.

He began slowing and looking about. Kathleen tried to tell herself not to panic—but she was. She decided the minute the car slowed enough to jump out she would open the door and bolt.

Finally the driver pulled into a small area beside the road. She clutched her purse and grabbed the door handle. It was locked! She was locked in, and Paulo the driver didn't seem to be in any hurry. Morbidly she wondered how many times he might have done this before. Casually he pulled a knife from above the visor and turned off the car lights.

Kathleen faced the door, her knees drawn up to her chin. First, he would have to get her out of the car, but she knew it would only be a matter of time before he would. He opened the door and grabbed at her ankles in an attempt to pull her out. She struggled, kicking to protect herself. She knew she couldn't stay in the car, but if he pulled her out by her feet she would end up on the ground with him over her.

As she fended off his attempts to pull her out she felt a sharp pain on her arm. In the melee his knife had grazed her forearm. The man soon realized that he was at a disadvantage. He had only one hand with which to pull her out—the other held the knife. Putting the flat side of the knife between his teeth he reached in with both hands.

Kathleen saw him coming. She recoiled then lashed out with her feet. One foot caught him in his chest and she felt the heel of her stiletto shoe slip between his ribs. It must have penetrated, for there was some resistance when she pulled her leg away.

He let out a guttural sound along with an expulsion of air and staggered backward. This was her chance and she seized it. Kathleen leaped from the car and dashed toward a row of bushes running along the road. She quickly glanced back. Doubled over trying to catch his breath he was hobbling after her.

She found a small opening in the bushes and squeezed through only to encounter another row. The reality of where she was became clear. These were grape vines—she was in a vineyard.

Trying to put as much distance as possible from her assailant she kicked off her shoes. They were unstable on the uneven ground and noisy on the stony path between the rows. In her bare feet she picked her way along the vines until she came to a little hole in the row. She crossed through and listened. A dog barked far off in the distance but there was no sound in the vineyard.

Then she heard it. It was him—the faint shuffle of footsteps and the sharp sound of a stone being overturned. She looked for openings in the rows large enough to squirm through. The twisted vines tugged grudgingly, scratching her and tearing at her dress. On she hurried, crossing many rows deeper into the vineyard.

Finally she could go no further and breathlessly sank down beside the grape vines and listened. She could hear her heart pounding and had lost all sense of time. A breeze stirred the leaves and a cloud skittered across the moon. Far off was a low moan of thunder. She listened for several more minutes. Kathleen had never felt more alone. She rubbed her bruised and painful feet. She had lost her shoes but she still had her purse.

Her purse! How foolish she had been. In her terror and panic she had completely forgotten about the gun in her purse. She was angry with herself...she had almost been killed by her thoughtlessness.

Kathleen opened her purse. The gun was cold but reassuring. She suddenly felt emboldened. Now, to find a way out—a farmer's cottage perhaps. Far ahead on the hillside she could see the end of the rows.

She limped toward it but soon came upon a narrow path cutting across the rows. It looked like a service road allowing the farmer to access his vineyard. This, she thought, might take her back to the country road winding down the valley. There would be houses along that road. She turned down the path and found the grassy strip easier going. Except for an occasional cloud the moon lit her way.

She walked for several minutes when, without warning, a figure appeared on the path ahead. He began advancing toward her. She stopped, motionless in her tracks and slipped off the safety of her little gun. He was no more than three rows away when she could see who it was. It was Paulo, the driver!

Even in the light of the moon she couldn't see the sights of the hand gun, but she was so close she didn't think it mattered. She continued to aim until he was only a few steps away and squeezed the trigger.

The gun jolted back and upwards, and the shot shattered the silence of the night. The man stopped abruptly. He stumbled to maintain his footing then fell backward into a row of grape vines. For an instant he hung there then, tumbled to the ground tearing down some of the vines with him.

Kathleen ran past him not pausing to look back. She wandered for some time. The ringing in her ears had faded and she could hear again. Far ahead a car door slammed...then another. A few minutes later she began to see tiny shafts of light skittering about—searching. She wasn't sure who they were until she heard urgent voices calling her name.

Kathleen called back and it wasn't long before she stood in in the beam of a flashlight held by a man she didn't know. After some comforting words of reassurance he called on his radio to report his discovery.

He escorted her back down the trail, his flashlight bobbing along the path. Ahead other lights began to converge. As they neared the other searchers Pepe stepped out from behind one of the lights and rushed toward her.

"Thank God you're all right," he said in a voice choked with emotion. He put a blanket and his arm around her and together they worked their way back toward the road.

"Pepe, I don't understand," she said tearfully. "You said I would be safe with René."

"That was not René, Kathleen. This man picked you up before René could get there. I'm so very sorry. I'm responsible. If anything bad had happened to you..." he broke off.

"Pepe, I shot the man!"

"I know. We heard the shot. Don't worry, he may not be dead, at least not yet. You may have only wounded him." He took the gun from her. "You won't need this anymore."

She sat beside Pepe in the back of a black limousine with two men in front. A second black car followed them. They passed the roadside area where it all began—there was no car there. It was if it had all never happened.

"We have to get you away from here,' said Pepe "but we need to decide where you want to go. We can take you back to your hotel or on to our villa. You'll be safe either place…"

She decided to go back to the Benedetti's. She was bloody from cuts and scratches, her hair was dirty and tangled and her party dress torn and muddy. It was now two-thirty in the morning. No, she would go back to the villa and clean up as best she could. Then, call her father first thing in the morning.

Kathleen was surprised to see the villa brightly lit. She did not see several men outside in the shadows—nor were they meant to be seen. She realized they had been expecting her. Someone must have called ahead.

In her nightgown and as elegant as ever Pepe's mother was waiting by the staircase. Her face clouded over in a motherly expression of concern when she saw Kathleen.

"Come here, my dear. You've been through enough for one night. Upstairs with me now, have to get you cleaned up." She put an arm around Kathleen and sternly waved away the other at the men. "Leave us alone! This will take a while." She took her to a guest bedroom and into the bathroom where Maria began to clean her cuts and scratches.

Kathleen was overcome by the care and concern of this woman. A woman she hardly knew. Attention she had seldom received from her own mother. She felt warm and secure. Her throat tightened. Tears appeared then, spilled over and down her cheeks.

"I'm sorry," she sobbed, her voice quivering with emotion. "This has been a nightmare—unreal. I can't believe it happened to me."

Maria nodded. "I understand. Believe me I do. Things like this rarely if ever happen to us women. It's our men we have to worry about." She wet another towel and turned back to her work. "Out from behind his work my husband is a good and gentle man. He desperately wants to retire and get as far away from this business as he can. He's tired of it, and he just wants to walk away from it and let the others fight over it—like vultures over a kill. However there's one man who wants it all and insists Antonio turn it over to him." She shook her head in disgust. "This man is very ambitious and cold. There is no blood in his veins. In my heart it is hard for me to hate anyone…but this may be the exception. May God forgive me!"

"Did he have that man try to kill me tonight?" asked Kathleen.

"No, I don't think so. As I said, women are off limits so to speak. Antonio thinks Fillipo—the man with the tattoo— realized you recognized him and might reveal his identity. He didn't know you already had. The driver must have been an accomplice."

Kathleen hesitated. She wasn't sure she should ask, but Maria seemed willing to confide in her. "Would this competitor kill to get what he wants?"

Maria closed her eyes. "Yes, he is capable of it and probably has, but so far with us it has only been threats and warnings if Antonio doesn't give him what he wants. Pepe is not involved in any way but being our son puts him at risk. That's why we called him back from New York." Maria appeared to look far off in the distance. "I worry so much…" she said twisting her hands.

Regaining her composure Maria stood and squared her jaw with a tight-lipped smile. "Now, I've put some clothes on the bed. Not too fashionable I'm afraid but comfortable—and I think they will fit you more or less. I'll turn on your shower…it takes a while for hot water. The plumbing is as old as this house. When you're done come down to the kitchen and I'll fix you something." She left calling over her shoulder "Then we should all try to get a few hours of sleep."

Chapter Eleven

She stirred…then her eyes flittered open. Kathleen blinked in the sunlight filling the room. For a few seconds she didn't realize where she was. Then the events of the previous evening came flooding back. She had overslept but was too comfortable and secure to do anything about it. She listened. The faint murmur of voices drifting from downstairs told her the house was up. She *must* get up.

She caught her breath…her father! This morning he would expect that she was back at the hotel. He would be calling her room—if he hadn't already. They had planned to spend the day visiting the Matisse and the Chagall Museum, as well as the Nice Museum of Fine Arts which displayed works of Monet, Renoir and Duffy. She dressed, and hurried downstairs following the voices to the kitchen.

"Good morning, my dear," said Maria jumping to her feet. "Grandmother and I were just talking about you. We decided to let you sleep after all that happened last night, some coffee, hot chocolate perhaps?"

"Le chocolat, s'il vous plaît," Kathleen replied, practicing her French. "I didn't mean to oversleep and I really need to call my father at the hotel. He will be trying to call my room if he hasn't already. We had planned to visit the museums today."

"Ah, *oui*…the museums," said grandmother, the customary blanket draped over her lap. We have a great many of them here in Provence. I've always thought it unfortunate that the great masters didn't paint anyone my age. Of course no one wanted to commission or sit for a portrait once they grew old. But I think some very interesting faces were missed, don't you?" She struck a fixed pose with an attempt at a sly Mona Lisa smile, then chuckled to herself.

Maria flipped through a phone book stopping suddenly to run her finger down the page. "Maybe its best if you don't alarm him with details of what happened last night until you can talk with him in person," she said handing Kathleen the phone. "You know how we worry about our children."

His room phone rang insistently until finally the hotel operator came back on the line. "I'm sorry, room two-twenty-seven is not answering. Would you care to leave a message?"

She did. "Hi, Dad. It's almost nine o'clock. I stayed at the villa last night. I'll tell you all about it when I see you. I expect to back there by ten-thirty or so. Love you. Bye."

Maria made the hot chocolate and set out some croissants and marmalade. "I'll have them tell Pepe—he wanted to know when you were up. He can take you into town."

It was a restless night for Kendall Campbell. He slept fitfully and now that the first rays of daylight began to illuminate his hotel room he was finally sleeping soundly.

The telephone on the bed stand rang twice before he realized where he was. Still disoriented he fumbled for the phone.

"Hello?"

"Is this Professor Campbell?"

"Yes…"

"Your daughter Kathleen decided to stay at the Benedetti house last night. It was getting late and she thought it best she stay. She's there now and would like you to join her. My name is François—a chauffeur for the family. I've been sent to get you. I'm on the road down to the city and will be at your hotel in fifteen minutes or so and will drive you back to the villa."

The foggy fingers of sleep had not yet released their grasp and Kendall was struggling to understand what he was hearing. "My daughter's at the Benedetti's and wants me to come there?"

"Yes," said the voice, "I'm sorry sir if I woke you. I'll be there shortly and will be waiting for you outside the hotel."

Kendall hesitated. "OK, all right. I'll be down as soon as I can."

He sat on the edge of the bed trying to make sense of it all. His head was clearing now. Why, he wondered, had Kathleen decided not to come back to the hotel. They had planned to visit the museums today. It was still early, maybe they still would. But what most perplexed him was why did she want him to come back to the villa? Why didn't she simply have the driver take her back to Nice?

Oh well, he shrugged, as he splashed cold water on his face—he would soon find out. Before leaving, on impulse he called her room in the hotel. There was no answer.

Outside the entrance to the Beau Rivage there were no cars at the curb. He stood for a moment before he turned to the right and something caught his eye. Half way down the block a man stepped from a black sedan and waved. As Kendall approached he held out his hand in greeting.

"Bonjour Monsieur, I am François your driver," he said with a disarming smile. "Allow me…"

As quickly as Kendall slid into the back seat the driver closed the door and in a matter of seconds they were off. As the car headed west along the coast on the *Promenade de Anglais,* Kendall felt vaguely uneasy. There was something about this François that he couldn't put his finger on. Then it came to him. Staring at the back of the drivers head he noticed that near his hairline there was a thin but distinct line where the color didn't match. The man, he realized, was wearing a wig. This, along with a bad moustache and sunglasses...

When they reached the roundabout the driver did not turn off onto the road up into the hills.

"Wasn't that our turnoff?" said Kendall trying to muster a commanding tone.

*Oui, oui...*if you don't mind I was told to get the car washed," he said pointing to a car wash at the end of the street. "There's no one in line and it'll only take a few minutes."

Kendall cautiously inched toward the door and casually put his hand on the door handle. The driver noticed his movement and glanced up in the rear view mirror. Kendall waited until the driver was occupied feeding money into the pay station to pull the door handle. To his dismay it did not yield. The chilling reality that the doors were locked supported his suspicions. However, he was somehow still reluctant to accept that he was in some sort of danger. Despite his intuition and better judgment he clung to the hope that this was all just a series of bizarre but harmless circumstances.

The car moved into position and was soon engulfed in an envelope of soapy spray. Without warning the driver whirled around and Kendall stared into the large black muzzle. He did not see it or hear it. Involuntarily he screamed as he was seized by an intense pain and burning sensation. His body was rigid and torn by muscle spasms then, within a few a seconds, he was consumed by a profound weakness.

He became aware of the man bending over him expressionless, his moustache askew. Kendall's senses returned to the point that he realized that he had been shot by a stun gun. In the dim interior of the sedan he saw the glint of a hypodermic syringe and faintly felt the sting of the needle in his arm.

Still powerless to move or struggle he drifted helplessly off into a pain-free darkness.

At first it was an incessant pounding. He thought it was his heart beating, but slowly the gaps between the beats began to fill with the whiney twang of a steel guitar. With considerable effort Kendall Campbell's eyelids managed to slide open. He squinted in the glare of a single overhead light. His head throbbed along with the music which was devoid of any discernible melody. Summoning the strength to sit up he was immediately met with an unyielding resistance. He fell back, breathing heavily and fighting to regain his senses.

Kendall lay there confused and disoriented. The frigid reality came slowly. He was in the middle of a wooden box with one wrist and one leg restrained by chains anchored into the floor. By positioning his body in a certain way he could sit up but not stand or reach the sides of the box. It was impossible to hear anything above the unrelenting music coming from a speaker mounted near a single light bulb in the top of the box.

Kendall had never suffered from claustrophobia, nevertheless he struggled to control a rising panic. He had no idea where he was other than he was confined to a box he estimated at about eight foot square. At one side just within reach sat a bucket and a small plastic bottle of water. At the other side there appeared to be a small opening cut into the side of the box. It was sealed closed. He assumed this provided access for his captors.

Kendall leaned back on his elbows and considered his plight. He remembered everything up until he was shot with the stun gun. The driver—François, or whatever his name—must have accomplices. What were their motives and more importantly what were their intentions, he wondered? And, why him?

Kathleen, he knew, would soon discover he was missing and she would be frantic.

His mind churned wildly. The kidnapping had been well planned. Not the work of amateurs. It would be difficult to trance his whereabouts. There must be some connection to the Benedetti family, he thought, although he doubted they were behind this for he and his daughter, along with the other Americans, had been so warmly received…besides, what possible motive would they have. Still, by sheer accident he had discovered the stolen Vermeer painting in the study. He hadn't had much time to examine it but he felt fairly sure that it was authentic. No one had seen him in the study. Of that he felt certain.

Unable to make any sense of it all he succumbed to the pounding in his head and lay back down. Kendall closed his eyes to not only shut out the glare of the light but also his surreal surroundings.

Pepe drove Kathleen back down to Nice and the Hotel Beau Rivage. Together they went to her room where she again tried to call her father. When there was no answer they went to his room and knocked on the door...there was no response. Pepe was more alarmed than Kathleen but he did not show it.

"Let's go down to the lobby," he said. "I'll see if I can get them to open the room."

"This isn't at all like him. He hasn't even called or left me a phone message. Pepe, I'm worried."

After some hesitation the assistant manager agreed to open Kendall's room and accompanied by the bellman on duty, the four of them opened the door. Kathleen held back, fearful of what she might find. The maid had not yet made up the room. The bed had obviously been slept in and his travel case, a few clothes on hangers and toiletry items were all as he might have left them. There was nothing unusual except the blinking message light on his phone from Kathleen's calls. It was as if this hotel guest had simply gone down for breakfast or out for the day.

"I'm sorry *Madame et Monsieur,*" said the assistant manager with a thinly disguised attempt to conceal his annoyance. "I have seen these things before and there is usually a perfectly logical explanation when the one in question reappears."

A few minutes later, Pepe called home to report Kendall was nowhere to be found, while Kathleen sat nearby on a sofa in the lobby.

"Let's stay around here for a while in case he shows up," suggested Pepe snapping shut his cell phone. "We can sit outside and have some lunch at one of the restaurants across the street."

It was sunny and comfortably warm for January, and under an umbrella Kathleen picked at a Niçoise salad while Pepe starred thoughtfully at his Compari and soda.

"We're going to have to go to the police, aren't we?" she said plaintively.

"Let's give it a few more hours," he replied. "Not enough time has passed for the police to take this seriously. Right now their response would be the same as the hotel manager." Pepe continued to stare at his drink. Finally he looked up. "Kathleen, it's very painful for me but there is something you must know. In Corsica my father was born into a family that had little respect for the law and French control of our country. Like many Corsican families they resented foreign domination of our island and struggled for freedom and sovereignty. We were separatists, but during World War II and the occupation of Corsica by Italian and then German troops we joined and became part of the French Resistance."

He swirled the ice around in his drink, considering how best to say what he knew he must. "It's a fine line between the violence of resistance in war and violence and lawlessness in peace time. Covert and clandestine activities of sabotage are easily adapted to the illegal activities of organized crime, and for many Corsican families it simply became a way of life."

Kathleen had stopped picking the tuna fish from her salad and stared intently at Pepe, afraid where this was leading.

"After the war my grandfather found it difficult to leave a life filled with threats and intimidation. Unfortunately it was expected that my father follow in his footsteps but he could not bring himself to be involved in activities in which violence was a requirement."

Kathleen's face was stern. "Are you telling me that your father is in organized crime?" She was incredulous that this old gentleman who had welcomed them into his home and had been so kind and gracious could be capable of such a thing.

Pepe looked sad and vulnerable and struggled for the words. "No...well...it's not what you think. Some things are within the law although they may be at the very edge. You must understand that here in France influence is an important factor in government and law enforcement. For example, in this country the government can't seize and confiscate criminal property and use it." He caught himself. He did not want to say too much. Swallowing hard, he continued. "Kathleen, my father is a good man. He has tried to leave behind his upbringing and the unsavory traditions of the Benedetti family. He wants to be left in peace and live out his old age with my mother."

Kathleen pushed aside her plate and they sat in silence. For months geography had separated them, but now there was different kind of space. She lowered her eyes. "Tell me," she said quietly "where do you fit in what your family calls 'the business'?"

"I don't! Father has always insisted I never be a part of it. I was always kept away. Even as a young boy I was sent away to a private school in Switzerland. I have never been exposed to it or involved in any way. Of course," he added "I will always be his son, and by association..." He broke off—looking intensely sad and vulnerable. Gone was the confident debonair man and only the boy tormented by his circumstances remained.

A sweet mixture of love and affection stirred in her, and Kathleen desperately wanted to hold and comfort him. "OK... I know that was hard to tell me but I needed to know...thank you." She put her hand on his. "Right now I need your help in locating my father. I'm getting frantic. Does this have anything to do with what you have just told me?"

"Maybe, my father thinks it does."

"First you get beaten in New York, then my attack last night and now my father's missing. It's all connected isn't it?"

"Yes, I'm afraid so." He took her arm reassuringly. "Don't worry Kathleen, we'll find him. In America the intent was just to hurt me and last night you likely would have been hurt but I don't think they would have killed you. It's the same with your father—we don't think his life is in danger."

Her eyes narrowed, she looked perplexed. "I don't understand…"

Killing people who aren't involved in a dispute doesn't accomplish anything except getting the attention of the authorities and the press, which would make matters worse. It's the *threat* of violence and intimidation—to get what they want. There's even a name for it. It's called *gambizzazione,* a warning."

"You say 'they', Pepe. Who are these people?"

"Its better I not tell you too much and I don't know everything myself.. In recent years ruthless men from Georgia, Chechnya and Russia have located here and are now responsible for much of organized crime in Southern France. It's called the Eastern Connection. One of these men, a Georgian, wants my father's enterprises as a cover for his high profile crime. Father has refused, of course, which has reportedly made this man furious."

"And this is the man behind what happened to me last night and may be responsible for my father's disappearance?"

"That is what we think." Pepe suddenly stiffened, quickly taking his cell phone from his pocket. "*Allo!*"

Kathleen intently studied his expression as he listened to the voice. It seemed interminable before he spoke.

"OK…yes, she's with me now. I won't let her out of my sight. I'll tell her…alright, be careful won't you. *Au revoir.*"

A rakish smile crossed his face. The vulnerable boy was gone. The man, confident and in control, was back. "That was father. The Georgian has contacted him and the man claims he had heard your father was missing. He would be happy to assure that he will be returned safe and unharmed if only my father would be reasonable and pass his business interests on to him. He would even be willing to pay a small sum. Father has agreed to meet with him to work out the details—sometime tomorrow."

"Then he *has* been kidnapped!"

"It looks that way. It's unlikely that the Georgian would have known he was missing unless he himself was responsible for it." Pepe paused to look casually around. "Don't worry, Kathleen, we'll get him back. In the meantime some of our family employees have been sent to make certain that we are safe. I see one across the street right now and another at the restaurant next door." He laughed. "Now you'll know what it feels like to be a bird in a cage."

He signaled the waiter for the bill. "Now, what do you say we walk towards the outdoor market. They will have closed up by now but we can walk down that way."

Hand in hand they strolled, passing restaurants with their chalkboards declaring the *menus du jour,* and pausing to look in the shop windows. Near the end of the *rue du Paule* they crossed over and walked along the sea wall. They walked in stride their arms now locked around each other's waist. Below on the pebble beach hardy sun bathers vied for patches of sand—topless women, men in their Speedos.

"Shouldn't we have told the men watching us where we were going?" she asked.

Pepe pulled her close. "You worry too much. They're close by. They are trained to be inconspicuous but I am so used to having them around I know where they are."

"Are you sure we shouldn't involve the police?" she asked apprehensively.

"Trust me, Kathleen. The police would bungle it up."

He had asked her before to trust him. And she had, and she did now. She wondered if it was her confidence and faith in him or her love...she wasn't sure. They made their way up the *Promenade des Anglais* lost in each other and their own thoughts

Finally, Kathleen turned to Pepe. "Do you think this *will* turn out all right—I mean my father being released unharmed?"

"I do. But it's a serious business. Anyway, it's our best option. You know, both of our father's lives are at stake here."

"Both?"

"My father feels that he is responsible for all of this. He said so on the phone. And he said he will do whatever is necessary to secure the safe release. It is very dangerous for him to meet face to face with the Georgian. However, once father has made up his mind it's impossible to change it and all I can do is ask him to be careful. Mother will be quite upset about it."

"Maybe he shouldn't do it."

"He has refused to deal with this man but now he feels he must give him what he wants. I'm just hoping the Georgian would rather be given it than take it. I couldn't bear to see anything happen to my father..."

For Kathleen the very thought was chilling. "Your father is risking his life to save my father's?"

Pepe shrugged again. There was nothing more to say...

†

He watched a spider in a corner of the box. Kendall studied the black speck hanging in its little web. They were both alone in their own world and he envied the spider. Unaware that it was captive in the box, he wondered if it was at all annoyed by the constant glare of the light and the incessant music.

Without warning, near the floor a small hatch opened and a tin plate slid through, then closed. It appeared to be some kind of sandwich along with slices of apple and a bottle of water thrown carelessly on top. He hadn't heard anyone coming—it was impossible with the music.

"Come back! Talk to me!" he cried, but there was no response.

He sat hunched over in misery. He had a myriad of questions. Who sent this driver to presumably take him back to the Benedetti villa? What could possibly be the motive for his kidnapping? Where was Kathleen and was she safe? One thing *was* clear—they had gone to considerable effort to kidnap him. It would have been far easier to have killed him. Whoever it was, wanted him alive.

His captors had taken his cell phone and all his identification. They had even removed his wrist watch and he had no conception of time. Kendall pondered how long he had been in the box—his best estimate was ten or twelve hours, but time here was elusive.

He wasn't sure he was hungry or eating might provide some relief from boredom. With some effort his arm and leg restraints allowed him to reach the plate with his fingertips and pull it close. It was two slices of coarse bread with a piece or two of bologna between. He ate every morsel.

Kendall had just picked up a slice of apple when he began to sense an inexplicable uneasiness. Nothing could be heard over the persistent beat of the music. He looked over at the spider. It hadn't moved, waiting patiently suspended in its web.

Then a tiny movement caught his eye. He closed his eyes then opened them, unsure of what he was seeing. At eye level and just beyond his reach an eye peered in through a knothole in the side of the box. It blinked. Kendall starred back.

"What are you doing in there?" said a small voice.

"I'm locked in here. Who are you?"

The eye disappeared.

"No! Don't go. Come back!" Kendall shouted in desperation. He starred at the little black hole…agonizing seconds passed. Then it reappeared.

"Don't go," he pleaded "please talk to me."

"Who are you?" said the voice.

Suddenly he realized it was a child's voice. "I'm a teacher—a nice man."

The eye continued to look back. Kendall desperately wanted to keep the child engaged.

"How old are you?' Kendall asked.

"Five."

"My name is Kendall. What's your name?"

"Alberto."

"I would like to be your friend, Alberto. Will you be my friend?"

"Why don't you have any friends? Are you a bad man?"

"I'm a good man, but I can't have friends here in the box."

"...I'll be your friend," said the boy.

"Good, I would like that. Do you live here?"

"I live here with my mother." He hesitated. "I've got to go now. I'm not supposed to be down here." The hole went black.

"Come back again! Come back and see me!' Kendall called after him and above the music. He watched the hole for some time but the eye did not reappear.

Antonio Benedetti shifted uneasily in his chair. Across from him sat Pepe, and Paulu Giordano. Giordano, despite being nearly Antonio's age, was a muscular well-built man who, except for a heavily weather-lined face, might have passed for much younger. Except for Antonio, he was seldom called by his real name but known as *Paulie il Guardiano*—or more simply, *"Il Guardiano"*..."The Guardian". Responsible for security, he had been with the family ever since Pepe could remember and had four full-time security men working for him along with another six on call.

Pepe could not recall The Guardian ever showing emotion and now he sat expressionless awaiting his instructions.

A stern Antonio addressed the two men. "If this is not resolved in the next twenty-four hours—say two o'clock tomorrow—we'll have no choice but to go to the police. I'm quite sure we have a better chance of getting this poor girl's father released unharmed than they do, but if I don't succeed we'll have no choice but to report it. In the meantime she will be safe here with Maria and Grandmother. Just as a precaution, Paulu, I would feel better if you had two men stay here with them. Pepe, how's Kathleen holding up?"

"Pretty good, considering all that's happened to her. She and her father are very close and understandably she's very worried."

"Does she trust us to get him back?"

"Yes, and she knows enough about the situation to be willing to wait before calling the police, but we can't expect her to wait much longer. She trusts me and believes that we will get him back. We can't let her down...I couldn't bear it."

"All right," said Antonio turning to The Guardian "here's what we are going to do and I don't have to tell you the consequences if it doesn't go according to plan."

The Guardian leaned forward expectantly as Antonio reached for the phone.

"Let's see if I can set it up with the Georgian." He punched in some numbers and sat back nervously tapping a pencil on his desk.

"*Allô*…this is Antonio Benedetti. I'd like to speak with *Monsieur* Branitski." Antonio stared straight ahead for what seemed an in ordinate amount of time. Suddenly he stiffened. "Stanislav, this is Antonio. It appears we have some things to talk about—an exchange of sorts. I'll give you my files and contacts with my blessing but I need to be assured that you can have this man freed unharmed."… "All right—but I have to talk to him in person once he's freed."… "OK, I'll meet with you but only on my terms. Not that I don't trust you of course, but for both of our safety." Antonio winked at the two men across from him, then, continued: "Listen carefully. I'll meet you at exactly noon tomorrow in the *La Castellane* area of Marseille. Just you and I and one other man each—unarmed of course. Give me a cell phone number and I'll call you at precisely eleven-thirty with the address. It will be a public place. If I see too many of your guys around, everything is off and I'll have no choice but to get the police involved. Messing with an American citizen presents problems I don't think you want right now. I'll give you everything you want but only on these conditions. Agreed?"

As Antonio listened a wry smile escaped from his pursed lips. What he was hearing was thinly veiled posturing and ego preserving admonitions, but he knew the Georgian would agree. "I think we understand each other," said Antonio "now let's get this done and over with. I'll call you at eleven-thirty tomorrow morning. *Au revoir.*"

He hung up and eased back in his chair with a sigh. His face looked worn and drawn. "This is why I want to retire and leave all this sordid business behind," he said wearily.

"Can you trust this Georgian?" asked Pepe.

""No!" his voice was tense "but as long as I give him what he wants and he can't be traced to the abduction there is no reason for violence. Unfortunately, he is not a reasonable and rational man."

"Why are we meeting him in Marseille?" asked The Guardian.

"I don't want to do it around Nice. A bird doesn't soil his own nest. Besides, things like this are not uncommon in Marseille—especially in the neighborhood of La Castellane where the police seldom if ever patrol. The meeting will be in a small restaurant—*Le Café Dragon*, at 85 Rue Dragon. Paulu, I want you with me. Arrange for a table off to the side, not in the middle. Get a parking space for the car near the entrance. Put some men around the outside the restaurant—they must be completely inconspicuous. Have another car and driver a few blocks away as well as one waiting in Nice to help retrieve Kathleen's father."

"What can I do?" asked Pepe.

His father shot him a stern glance. "Stay here! Watch the women and be our contact with the villa. In the meantime, keep Kathleen occupied. Reassure her and give her the attention and affection she needs right now."

It sounded like an appealing idea to Pepe.

†

He had been sleeping soundly but now his body ached from the hard floor of the box and the cramped position he was forced to lie in. Kendall thought he had been asleep for quite some time but he couldn't be certain. It occurred to him that there might have been a sedative in his food or water, but then again maybe it was exhaustion from his ordeal.

A plate with a slice of cheese, a piece of sausage and bread sat at the end of the box. The bread was dry and the cheese curled up at the edges. It had obviously been there for some time,

He became aware of a tapping that was not synchronous with the beat of the music. The eye was back!

"Alberto, is that you?"

"Yes…"

"I'm so glad you came to visit me again. Do you know what time it is?"

"…No."

"Then do you know what day it is?"

"Wednesday. My mother always works in the morning on Wednesday."

"Who else is in the house?"

"What?"

"Are you alone in the house now?"

"Yes—until she gets back."

"Alberto, look around you. I'm locked in here—do you see a key anywhere?"

The boy's eye remained framed in the hole. "No...why?"

"Alberto, you didn't look!"

"It's not down here. Vadim keeps it upstairs on a hook."

"Who is Vadim?"

"My mother's boyfriend, sometimes he lives here."

"Can you get it and show it to me—through the hole I mean?"

He hesitated. "I don't want to be bad. I'm not supposed to be down here, you know."

"Alberto, listen to me. You're not bad, you're a good boy. You're my friend and that's what a friend would do. We're friends, right? Show me the key."

"Alright...stay here."

Kendall smiled. He thought he could hear the boy's legs clamoring up the steps. Now it seemed warmer in the box. His palms were moist and tiny beads of sweat dampened his forehead. He was putting the boy's welfare, even safety in jeopardy but the thought of being able to do something about his confinement was overpowering.

The tantalizing tip of a key wiggled in the knot hole, then withdrew to be replaced by an eye.

"Good job, Alberto! Can you push it through the hole for me?"

Again the boy hesitated, conflicted and uncertain. Then the key reappeared in the hole—then farther, until it dangled inside the box from a string. Another key entered tied together with the first. Two keys dropped into the box with a sound mostly muffled by the music.

Kendall's heart sank when he realized that the keys were beyond his reach. The chains of his restraints were unyielding and he was inches short of being able to retrieve the keys. Freedom lay just beyond his grasp.

The plate…perhaps the little tin plate could help him reach an extra six or eight inches. It did. By reaching out with the plate he could touch one of the keys, but it slipped off. Again he tried. He had been concentrating so much on the keys that he had forgotten about the boy. He looked up at the knot hole. He was gone. "Alberto! Alberto, are you there?" There was no response and the eye did not come back.

Kendall worked feverishly. Each time he was able to move the keys a bit closer on the next attempt he pushed them farther away. In the back of his mind was the nagging realization that time was critical.

On one attempt he was able to catch the rim of the metal plate on the serrated edge of a key. Slowly, maintaining a steady pressure, he pulled the keys within reach. Quickly he slipped a key into the lock on his wrist and with little resistance it turned and snapped open. Assuming the other key was for his ankle lock he pushed it into the cylinder. It entered with ease and when turned the lock popped open.

Clear of his chains he was now able to move freely within the box. The container was reasonably sturdy and appeared to have been some type of shipping crate. Somehow he had to force his way out. The music would stifle most of any sound. Hunched over, his head grazing the ceiling, he put his shoulder against the door. It yielded somewhat but did not give way. Kendall stepped back, braced himself, and kicked the side of the crate as hard as he could.

To his surprise the wood splintered and the door fell open, now hanging loosely by one hinge. In the dim light of the cellar Kendall bolted for the stairs. He paused at the top and listened…on the other side of the door he heard strange little voices punctuated with musical sounds. He had no choice. Slowly he opened the door.

There, sitting on a well-worn couch was Alberto, intently watching cartoons on a little television screen. There was no one else in sight. When Kendall entered the room Alberto seemed startled but not afraid.

"Here," said Kendall handling him the keys, "put them back where you got them. Maybe no one will ever know how I got out." He took the little hand in his and shook it. "Thank you Alberto, you are the best friend anyone could have. I'll never forget you…good luck!"

Out of the corner of his eye Kendall saw Bugs Bunny with a carrot hurriedly disappear down a hole. He had better quickly disappear himself.

The Guardian had done his work. Arrangements for the meeting with the Georgian were complete. He had gone to *Le Café Dragon* to check out the layout of the restaurant. It was patronized principally by locals, but also frequented by those outside the neighborhood who found themselves in the area for reasons both legitimate and nefarious. Directly across the street was an empty shop and for an attractive fee The Guardian was able to make arrangements with the leasing company to "inspect" the building prior to making a commitment to rent it. Early in the morning of the meeting, several "workmen" arrived in their van and were busily engaged in carrying building materials and tools to and from their truck. Meanwhile, a car and its driver were parked directly in front of the restaurant—preserving the parking space for the arrival of Antonio and The Guardian. A few doors down at a bus stop a middle-aged couple waited, but the busses that stopped never seemed to be the one they were waiting for. Everything was in place.

A few minutes before eleven-thirty Antonio arrived. As his car approached the restaurant the car parked in front of the entrance pulled away and The Guardian parked in its place.

Antonio lifted the cover of his cell phone and dialed the number. "...Stanislav? I'll meet you at *Le Café Dragon* at *85 Rue Dragon*. I'm almost there now. I'll get a table for us. I'll have one man with me as we agreed. Are you sure you can deliver your part of the bargain? ...Good. Let's get this done. Meet you there."

The Guardian scanned the room as they entered the restaurant. It was still early and mid-day patrons had yet to arrive. A waiter bent over a table writing the *menu du jour* in chalk on a menu board. One other table was occupied by two elderly women, while three grizzled men sat hunched over the bar. The Georgian had only learned of the meeting place a few minutes ago but you could never be too careful.

Antonio took a table off to the side while The Guardian strolled casually to the bar. The bartender saw him coming.

"Can I get you something?" said the man wiping his hands on a towel.

"Two pastis,…water on the side."

The bartender nodded, "Ice?"

"No ice."

The bartender took down a bottle of the dark amber liqueur and began filling the glasses.

The Guardian gestured to the three men at the end of the bar. "Regulars?" he asked.

"Yes—more regular at the beginning of the month when they get their public assistance." He slid two glasses across the bar. "I'll bring the water to your table," he said turning to the cooler.

Antonio sat stoically at the table, some notebooks and ledgers at his side.

"A menu, perhaps?" asked the bartender setting a bottle of water on the table.

"No, at least not now," said Antonio "we're expecting two others."

Antonio filled the glasses with water turning the mixture a milky yellow. Lifting his glass he and The Guardian touched their glasses—in anticipation that there would be a favorable outcome.

✝

Kendall stepped out of the house and was surprised to find that the entrance was off an alley. The alley, barely wide enough for a car, was a clutter of garbage cans, old cars and a wide array of discarded items and litter. A dog lying in the shade of a trash bin eyed him warily. Several blocks to the south he could not see beyond the tall non-descript housing complexes crowding the skyline.

Anxious to get away from the house his impulse was to run but he knew it might attract attention. Kendall quickly walked down the alley until it opened onto a street lined with single-stored shops and businesses heavily protected by security bars and grating on the windows and doors. He stopped momentarily to look around. There was a laundromat, an auto parts store, liquor store, and a small neighborhood convenience store with an overhead sign in Arabic script. A woman wearing a head scarf and an ankle length thawb approached with two young children in tow. Before she reached him she crossed the street in what he thought was a cautious but obvious effort to avoid him.

Kendall looked at himself. Not only did he feel out of place here but he was unshaven with uncombed hair—and clothes that looked like they had been slept in, which of course they had.

A taxi cab rounded the corner and turned onto his street. He waved wildly and the cab driver pulled over and looked out his window expectantly.

"Can you take me to Gattiéres?" Kendall had no idea where he was. He knew he was still in France—the street and store signs assured him of that. Going back to the Benedetti villa in Gattiéres seemed as good a place as any. They would know what to do and would, without question, pay his taxi fare.

"Where?" asked the driver rubbing his chin apprehensively as he looked at this disheveled man who was clearly out of his element.

"Gattiéres..a little village in the hills above Nice."

"Oh...*Gattiéres*!" said the cab driver in a decidedly Provençal pronunciation. "No go there." With an expression of irritation and shaking his head he sped off.

Kendall had no money and no identification. He looked desperately up and down the street for a public pay phone. Maybe, he thought, an emergency call could be made with requiring money or a phone card—but there was none in sight. Hopeful that that there may be one in the convenience store he crossed the street and entered.

Behind the counter an inscrutable woman looked at him blankly.

Summoning up his courage and his best French he asked: "Is there a pay phone around here?"

A disdainful smile parted her lips revealing several missing teeth, "You won't find any around here. So much theft and vandalism they took them out years ago."

Do you have a phone I could use then? Just for a quick call?"

Her face darkened. "We only have one phone here and it's not for customers."

"Can you make an emergency call for me?"

"An emergency call...to who?"

"The police."

"The police! Her lips tightened and her eyes narrowed. "We don't want the police here. Get out!"

Kendal turned away and the next customer stepped to the counter. Disillusioned and alone he headed for the door when a hooded figure intercepted him. It was the woman in the head scarf with the two children. He now realized that she hadn't crossed the street to avoid him but to cross to the store.

"You're not French, I can tell from your accent. English, perhaps?"

I'm American, actually."

"Ah, I should have known. I went to school at Michigan State,' she said in near perfect English.

Kendall could scarcely believe what he was hearing. He thought the young Muslim woman with flawless taffy-colored skin to be of North African origin. She had large dark eyes and a friendly smile. Momentarily distracted by her restless children she quieted them with a few words in a language he didn't recognize.

Turning back to Kendall she asked: "Are you in some kind of trouble?"

"Yes. I desperately need to make a phone call."

"Here," she said reaching into her bag "you can use my cell phone. What's the number?"

"Well that's part of the problem. I don't really know. It's a family who live in the hills above Nice…a place called Gattiéres."

"I know the village. Maybe I we can look it up…here hold this," she said handing him her shopping basket.

She began to exchange harsh words with the store clerk when a man appeared behind the counter. A heated exchange continued with the man, who began gesturing angrily Again, it was not a language that Kendall could understand but he knew the context of the confrontation.

Finally the young woman took her basket from Kendall and dropped it on the counter. With a look of disgust the man waved his hands in resignation and produced a large phone book from under the counter.

"Sorry," she said turning to Kendall "the trouble is people don't want to get involved, they're intolerant and only concerned for themselves."

She studied the directory. "Good, the Gattiéres area is included. Now, what's the name of the person you want to call?"

"Benedetti."

"First name,,,?"

"Antonio."

"Her head snapped up. "Antonio Benedetti!" she cried. "I know him…well not personally, but I have heard of him," Her demeanor changed almost imperceptibly. "How do you know him?"

"I don't really. I've only met him once. My daughter and his son are friends."

"Well, let's see if he is listed," she said her fingers running down the pages. "I know of the Benedetti family because I was born in Corsica. My people, the moors, controlled the island centuries ago but we are the minority now—only about ten per cent of the population there. As Muslims there was a great deal of hatred and violence directed at us and we did not want to raise our children there. Many other Muslim families have come from Corsica to Marseilles and there is now a small community of us. We are struggling here, but we don't want to go back."

Kendall was shocked. He was in Marseille!

"Ah, we're in luck'" she said as she began to dial. She slipped the phone under her head covering and listened, as Kendall watched anxiously.

"Yes, is this the Benedetti residence? I'm calling for Antonio Benedetti…who's calling?.. hold please"…

Kendall took the phone. "This is Kendall Campbell. Who am I speaking to?" Relief flooded his face. "Pepe!"

Chapter Twelve

As a rule security men are inconspicuous and blend into their surroundings, but this man was clearly the exception. Stanislav Branitski's bodyguard was an a man who might immediately attract attention or even arouse suspicion. He was a giant of a man, a huge brutish looking fellow. He lumbered into *Le Café Dragon*, paused for a few seconds then walked directly to Antonio's table.

"*Monsieur* Benedetti—if you don't mind, I have

been asked by *Monsieur* Branitski to insure that the facilities here are appropriate for the meeting. He is outside and will be here as soon as I can make sure things are in order." He looked casually around then headed to a little hallway leading to the restrooms. He disappeared into the men's room, quickly reappeared, and then went into the women's room next to it. A few moments later he reentered, and as the bartender peered over the rim of his eyeglasses with a mixture of curiosity and suspicion, the security man, looking neither right nor left, waddled out of the restaurant.

The Guardian chuckled. "I guess He doesn't trust you. Does he think he has anything to fear from you?"

"Violence is how he has always done things," replied Antonio "brutality is the only way he knows. Being so cautious is probably why he is still alive."

When the Georgian and his bodyguard entered it was clearly apparent which one was Stanislav Branitski. Neither discreet nor inconspicuous, he wore Italian designer shoes and a shiny hand tailored suit with a colored shirt and matching pocket handkerchief—all accentuated by a paisley tie. He looked completely incongruous in a little neighborhood restaurant in a poor suburb of Marseilles. The man himself was unmemorable. A rotund belly obscured any evidence of a belt on his pants, and a flaccid face barely accommodated two small eyes. He was afflicted with an occasional facial tic which twitched without warning.

After feeble attempts at greetings and introductions the four men sat facing each other. It was an uncomfortable moment and it was at this time that

Antonio first noticed the Georgian's facial tic. Although slight, it involuntarily pulled one corner of his mouth into a quick but fleeting sneer, especially when he seemed nervous or under stress.

"We are having a pastis." said Antonio lifting his glass "would you care to join us?"

No," replied the Georgian signaling the waiter "but I *will* have a cognac."

The waiter hurried to the table.

"A bottle of Ararat cognac."

"…Ararat?"

"It's Russian—Armenian actually. The best in the world." said the Georgian.

The waiter winced. "I'm sorry *Monsieur*, but I'm quite certain we don't have it. We have some very nice French cognac."

The Georgian wrinkled his nose, "Then bring a bottle of the best you have."

"A *bottle, Monsieur*?"

"A bottle! A bottle!"

The waiter shrugged. "Very well."

During this exchange The Guardian had been studying the Georgian's bodyguard. There was something about the man that troubled him. Not only did he not *look* like a bodyguard, he wasn't *acting* like one. He didn't seem to have any awareness or concern of what was going around him. Moreover, he was a small thin man with a pinched face and a pencil thin moustache. An odd man and someone you would naturally distrust.

The waiter returned with a bottle of cognac for the Georgian's approval. He examined it, turning it about in his fleshy hands. Then, with an expression of distain, he nodded his acceptance.

Suddenly, Antonio felt his cell phone vibrating in his pocket. Surely, he thought, everyone knew not to call him now…unless it was urgent. Looking annoyed he excused himself and flipped open the cover. He recognized the number that was calling and pressed the phone tightly to his ear. "*Allo?*"

"Can you hear me?" the voice said.

"Yes…"

"This is Pepe. Campbell escaped on his own. They may or may not yet know that he is missing. He called from a convenience store in the north of Marseille not far from where you are. Can you believe it? Anyway, I've already called the car you had stationed near you and they're on the way to pick him up. They should be there within the next ten minutes. I know you probably can't talk right now but keep your phone on vibrate. I'll call you when they have him—you don't have to answer. Be careful!"

Antonio tried his best to maintain an annoyed expression. "Listen, you called me at a bad time. Tell him I'll get back to him next week. He'll have to wait. Don't call me again. I'm busy right now."

While Antonio was on the phone the Georgians' bodyguard excused himself to go to the restroom. The Guardian watched him as he walked to the back hallwayl, but to his surprise the man went in the wrong door and disappeared into the women's room. Odd, perhaps a mistake, but things like this attracted The Guardian's attention.

"Well," said Antonio sipping his pastis "shall we enjoy our drinks before we get down to business?"

The Georgian pointed to the neatly bundled stack of documents at Antonio's elbow. "As long as you've brought everything I need—I'll have to take a quick look at them of course".

"You have yet to deliver your part of the bargain," replied Antonio evenly.

The bodyguard returned from the restroom when a beefy man entered the restaurant and hurried to their table. It was the Georgian's huge security man. "Pardon, *Monsieur* Branitski may I have a word with you?"

In a corner nearby they spoke in Ukrainian in hushed tones. Antonio watched them intently over the rim of his pastis. He suspected that they had discovered that Kendall had escaped and the Georgian's reaction might confirm it. As the Georgian listened his eyes grew wide, then, narrowed as his face began to twitch in a violent series of spasms. Barely able to control his anger he whispered a few tense instructions and returned to the table as the man left the restaurant.

"I'm afraid there's been a change of plans," he said while adjusting his tie in a prearranged signal to the bodyguard. The little man quickly produced a handgun, pointing it at Antonio.

"Don't move!" commanded the Georgian as he snatched the documents from the table. "I'm sorry it had to come to this." He turned, and following closely on the heels of his security man he hurried for the door.

With both hands The Guardian shoved the table violently into the bodyguard tipping him over backwards and crashing to the floor. In a flash The Guardian was on him wrestling for control of the gun. It discharged and the struggle continued. The little man was clearly no match for the strength of his opponent and The Guardian was able to twist the handgun into the bodyguard's chest. He squeezed the man's finger on the trigger. The blast sent the bodyguard reeling backwards where he slumped to the floor.

The bartender crouched behind his bar speaking urgently into a phone. Customers cowered under tables or huddled in corners.

Antonio grabbed The Guardian by the arm. "Paulu, we have to get out of here!"

"I can't," he groaned, clutching his stomach. He reached out to Antonio with a bloody hand. "Here…here are the keys. Take the car—hurry!"

Antonio hesitated but The Guardian waved him off. "Go, you've got to get out of here," he said weakly.

Antonio ran to the door and into the street, blinking in the sunlight. Outside the restaurant it was seemingly a normal day on the *Rue Dragon* with no indication of the chaos and terror inside. In his pocket his cell phone was vibrating, and he smiled.

He stepped off the curb and was opening the driver's door when he heard the sharp whine of a motor scooter rapidly slowing down. Two riders, similarly dressed, wore dark clothing and black helmets with tinted face shields. Instantly he knew the implications. As they came alongside the passenger turned toward Antonio who was desperately trying to get safely behind the armored protection of the car door.

It was too late... The crack of an automatic weapon broke the relative quiet of *Rue Dragon* as the motor scooter slowed. The two people at the bus stop started running toward the scene. The motor scooter tried to speed up as one of the workmen across the street returned fire back from the back of his van. The driver was hit and lost control, sending the motor scooter over the curb where it jackknifed and crashed into the window of a *pâtisserie.*

The scene was bizarre, even surreal. The motor bike and its riders lay in a tangle of contorted arms and legs half inside the shop window. Along with the window, glass display shelves were shattered. Some still hung precariously, their contents spilling to the floor. Colorful fruit tarts of raspberry, peach and cherry lay on and around the riders. Croissants appeared here and there. A crème filled pastry had left a comet-like trail across the face shield of one of the helmets, while a wheel of the motor bike turned, slowly losing its momentum. The wail of sirens could be heard in several directions.

Close by, Antonio lay on the pavement with one leg in the car. He had almost made it. There was an ugly dark spot on the side of his head and from it a little rivulet of blood began slowly working its way down the grimy street.

†

At one end of the great room in the Villa Benedetti the four waited anxiously while outside two security men patrolled the grounds.

Pepe paced, never more than a few feet from the phone. Kathleen sat nearby nervously twisting her hands in her lap. Maria, stoic as ever, had made cool drinks and little assorted sandwiches, and toying with one on her plate. Grandmother, of course, always cold, sat with a blanket across her knees.

The first call was from the car sent to retrieve Kendall at the convenience store. Pepe leaped to answer it. "*Allo*, Pepe."

"Pepe, there has been trouble here," said the voice clearly agitated and out of breath. "Antonio has been hit. The police and an ambulance are here—another ambulance is just arriving. They're taking him to *Les Ventre de Traumatologic* here in Marseilles. Pepe…it doesn't look good. We have shot two of theirs. I haven't been inside the restaurant yet…and I don't know where The Guardian is. Have to go—its chaos here."

Pepe slowly returned the phone to its receiver while contemplating what he would say to the women. "There was trouble and father was shot."

A little gasp involuntarily escaped from Maria. The women anxiously hung on his every word.

"He's been taken to *Les Centre de Traumatologic* in Marseilles...it sounded like it was not good but we won't know for certain until we get there. Kathleen, you stay here with grandmother and wait for your father. You'll both be safe here. Mother and I will head to the hospital—I'll have one of the men bring a car around right away. I'll have to drive because I want to leave both security men here. They need to be on alert and I'm going to ask them to break out some automatic rifles until we know what's going on. The Georgian's gone crazy—is he trying to start a war between us? I'll have the car that was stationed in Nice intercept us along the way to Marseille and that will give us two cars so mother and I have security."

Pepe bounded out the door. The confidence and self-assurance with which he was taking command of the situation did not go unnoticed by Kathleen...nor by his mother. For Maria it was unsettling. Pepe had always been sheltered from the unsavory machinations of the family business, and Maria and Antonio had taken great care in doing so. Now, Maria thought, he was acting a lot like his father.

On the road to Marseille the car with Kendall and the car with Pepe and Maria passed each other. They maintained frequent contact by cell phone, and from reports in Marseille it was learned that The Guardian had also been shot but was alive in serious condition. Also, two unidentified men were dead at the scene after crashing their motor scooter into a store front and a third, identified as Boris Aleksandrov, was found dead inside a nearby restaurant of an apparent gunshot wound. One of the local television stations reported that Aleksandrov was known to be an associate of crime boss Stanislov Branitski and they speculated that this was an organized crime dispute over control, although police would not confirm it.

It was about two and a half hours from Marseille to the villa in Gatttiêries and for Kendall Campbell it seemed an eternity. He was only able to glean fragments of the conversation between the two security men in the front seat and he could only determine that there had been some kind of trouble at a restaurant in Marseille and the two security men seemed quite concerned.

Kendall was exhausted, but now he felt safe and secure and an overwhelming sense of relief. He leaned his head back on the leather seat. His mind wandered. His eyes began to focus on nothing in particular passing by. The outside soon became a blur. He caught himself dozing a few times … then succumbed and allowed himself to drift off to sleep…

Again Kendall heard music, but this time it was far off in the distance and as sweet and heavenly as ambrosia. It was a violin, more beautiful than he had ever heard and he felt inextricably drawn to it. His daughter—yes, it must be Kathleen, and the music would lead him to her.

It was twilight and he was in an unfamiliar place. He stood on a cobblestone street and shivered, there was a chill in the air. There was no one in sight and no movement except for the flicker of a lantern in the second floor window of a shop across the street. The little window was all but closed against the brisk air of late autumn, but from it he recognized the melody from Vivaldi's Four Seasons Concerto. It was the violin part of the first movement—"Spring", and one of Kathleen's favorites. She could, in fact, play it by memory.

Kendall thought he must be in a very old part of a city or town for the buildings were dark and stained with age and the street was gloomy and rank. Directly across the street and a few inches above a worn threshold was a door identified as no.7, and in a window above the doorway dulcet tones beckoned him. The compulsion to find his daughter was overpowering and all consuming. Putting fear aside, he found the door unlocked and entered. The interior smelled of fresh-cut wood and varnish. Following the sound of the violin, in semi-darkness he felt his way up a stairway and cautiously entered the room at the top.

By the light of the lantern and several candles placed about the room he immediately recognized the slender form of Kathleen. She was standing with her back to him, playing her violin with a passion and tenderness that wrung a sanguine sweetness from every note. She had tucked her blond hair beneath a cap, with errant wisps trailing down the back of her neck. She finished playing and lowering her fiddle from between her cheek and shoulder she turned to him.

This was not Kathleen! A pleasant enough face perhaps, even attractive, with Nordic features, but her woeful blue eyes seemed to look beyond Kendall as if he wasn't there.

Unsure whether he should apologize and excuse himself or just run, he glanced quickly around the room. In the dim light of flickering candles he could make out the figure of a man lying on a bed. The man's eyes were closed and his face drawn.

Frightened, Kendall looked back at the woman. With boney fingers she seductively held out the violin to him. Her face had contorted into a death mask with a mouth arched in a mocking smile. Cold fingers of terror gripped him. He yelled—but there was no sound. He felt himself falling ...

†

Kendall toppled to the side, jarring him awake. The car had arrived in Gattiêries and turned sharply onto the narrow streets. The dream, still vivid, left him uneasy.

Kathleen was waiting under the portico when the car turned off the country road and onto the driveway. In seconds they flung themselves into each other's arms—father and daughter.

"I was so worried about you," she sobbed, unable to say more.

"I was pretty worried myself. I'll tell you all about it, but not now. Right now I don't want to talk or even think about it. Besides...what's going on here?
Is there some kind of trouble?"

"You don't know?"

"No one has told me anything, but listening to the men who drove me here I can tell something is wrong."

Kathleen took him by the arm and led him into the house. "There's only me and Grandmother here and I should check on her. Oh, Daddy, terrible things have happened!"

When Grandmother saw Kendall she reached out for him and took both of his hands in hers. She held them tightly, looking up from her wheelchair with watery dark eyes. He felt that she was telling him something that words could not express.

Finally she said "I am so sorry that this sordid business happened to you. And now,'" she looked away "I am losing my son. May God have mercy!"

Kendall turned to Kathleen, questioningly.

"Mr. Benedetti has been shot and it's quite serious. Maria and Pepe have gone to the hospital in Marseille. They are there now.."

Still holding Grandmother's hands he knelt beside the lady. Her cold blue-veined hands had relaxed their grip and she turned her head slightly. The eyes were sad and focused on something far away. She nodded to herself. "One enemy is too many and a hundred friends not enough, and he who sups with the devil must have a long spoon."

Kendall gently squeezed her hands "Grandmother Benedetti, I'm very sorry. Maybe your son is not as badly injured as first thought."

She smiled a sad smile. "Thank you for your kindness. I suppose you could say it's a mother's intuition or maybe the insightful premonitions that come with old age, but in reality it's neither. It's just common sense.

They would have called from the hospital by now unless Antonio is dead. It must be that Pepe and Maria are on their way back because that is something they must tell me in person." She exhaled a little sigh. "I had always hoped that our little son would not follow in his father's footsteps. But it was a hard life then in Corsica. When walking in deep snow it is much easier to walk in the footsteps of the one ahead. Now I fear Pepe, my grandson, will be the next to follow—and only sadness and tragedy lie waiting."

Kendall stood and she straightened the little blanket on her lap. "I think I'd like to be alone, if you don't mind, while we wait for them to return." She swiveled her wheelchair around and slowly made her way out of the room.

Grandmother was right. Pepe and Maria returned with red-rimmed eyes and grim faces. Antonio, essentially dead at the scene, died shortly after being brought to the hospital.

The consequences of his death were swift and immediate. Security staff and other employees were uncertain and in disarray for they no longer had anyone to make assignments and give them direction. And so they turned to Pepe.

He gathered Kathleen, Kendall and his family into the library. "I don't yet have all the details," he said, "but I know that father was apprehensive about meeting with the Georgian and he took precautions. He chose what he thought was a secure meeting place and the Georgian wasn't told where it was until a half hour before. He didn't want to give them time to set up an entrapment. Several of our security men and women were stationed at a nearby bus stop and others posed as workmen across the street. There was a car posted in Nice and one in Marseilles to pick up Kendall wherever he might be released."

Kendall nodded. "I wondered how they got there so fast."

"Paulie..."The Guardian" was with father in the restaurant," Pepe continued "but as previously agreed he was not armed. According to Paulie, before the Georgian arrived one of his security men came in and under the pretense of making sure the restaurant was secure hid a hand gun in the women's restroom—probably in the baby changing station or under the sink. Then the Georgian's bodyguard, known to be one of his enforcers, excused himself and retrieved the gun just prior to their learning that Kendall had escaped." Pepe paused, running his hands through his hair. Clearly it was painful to recount what he had learned.

Kendall shifted uneasily in his chair. "Then when I escaped it changed everything?"

"Yes, I think so. We think the Georgian had decided that if he didn't get what he wanted he would resort to force. When he learned that you had escaped he no longer had any advantage and he knew father would no longer be forced to agree. With father dead he could forcibly take over our business."

Kendall sat silently and looked very uncomfortable. Finally he said quietly "I have the impression that Antonio would never have agreed to meet with this man if I was not being held hostage."

A grim smile broadened Pepe's face. "Yes, he felt responsible for both the attempt on Kathleen's life and your abduction. He would have given this man anything he wanted in exchange for your release. He knew it was very dangerous to meet with him but my father was willing do whatever was necessary to get you back unharmed."

"Then," Kendall said softly "he risked his life to save mine."

Pepe shrugged. "That was the kind of man he was."

For the first time Maria spoke. "He was able to avoid the assassination attempt in the café, but despite all his precautions he could not escape entrapment on the street." She looked and Kendall, then Kathleen. "I am so sorry you became involved in this family affair. We opened our home and our hearts to you…and it has come back to haunt us all."

Grandmother stiffened. Her distant gaze vaporized and she turned her watery eyes to Maria. "We can't be haunted by the ghost of what might-have-been, my dear. The past is no longer within our reach. Now we need to be concerned about what is yet to come." She turned to her grandson. "Pepe, it's tempting to walk in the footsteps of the one who has gone before…please be careful where you go now."

Chapter Thirteen

The bells tolled laboriously in the bell tower of S. Nicholas Church in Gattiéres. A solemn cluster of black shrouded men eased the coffin of Antonio Benedetti down the steps of the thirteenth century church.

Kendall, anxious to put the whole experience behind, desperately wanted to return to Boston. But he couldn't. He knew he must stay and pay his respects to the man who had lost his life trying to save his. He and Kathleen watched as a solemn line of cars left the churchyard and snaked their way under the stark canopy of plane trees lining the road to the ancient cemetery of Guitéries.

Kendal and Kathleen went back to the villa to await the return of the Benedetti family and to spend their last night in France. They were leaving for home in the morning.

Kathleen was both confused and conflicted. Pepe now seemed preoccupied with his new responsibilities as head of the family and he was strangely distant. On the few occasions in which they had a few moments together neither of them seemed willing to talk about what effect the tragic circumstances seemed to be having on their relationship.

The father and daughter sat solemnly on the patio overlooking the valley stretching out to meet the Mediterranean in the distance. Lost in their own thoughts neither spoke.

One of the house staff, a pleasant young woman, appeared in the doorway. "Is there anything I can get you?" she asked in the rich Provençal accent of the south of France. She didn't appear to be a maid or housekeeper, and in fact she wasn't. She was one of the security people assigned to watch over the two Americans.

"No, I think not, thank you," replied Kendall.

The woman nodded and quietly disappeared.

"Kathleen," said her father quietly "are you ready to go home tomorrow?"

"Yes…that is, I know we must if only for our own safety."

"I meant having to say goodbye to Pepe."

"In a way I want to stay here with him. He needs me now and he has always been there for me, but I don't know what I could do to help him. Besides, he seems so distant now. I don't know what to think. It makes me so sad."

"I know. This whole thing has been a nightmare and both of us could have been…" he broke off. "This is not for us, Kathleen. We are out of our league here."

A scurry of activity announced the arrival of the family from the internment. In a few moments Pepe appeared on the patio and sank into a chair beside them.

"This was an incredibly hard day," he said wearily. "Now mother thinks he should have been buried in our family cemetery on Corsica. Both she and my father grew up there. Times were harder there, but nevertheless happier and more carefree. She thinks he should be returned to his native land and grandmother agrees. Come spring we will probably rebury him there."

Kendall nodded. "We are most comfortable in familiar surroundings. There is always a compelling urge to be where we are most at home."

Kathleen lowered her eyes. "There is a chill in the air. I think I'll go in."

"You're right," agreed Pepe. "The sun goes down early this time of year. It'll be dark soon. I think mother is in the kitchen fixing us a little something to eat."

Despite the tragic loss of the patriarch of the family the Benedetti's were warm and hospitable. Maria served up an onion soup followed by pan bagnat sandwiches.

Grandmother, stoic as ever, seldom spoke, and when she did it was brief and pertinent.

At the end of the meal Pepe took Kathleen by the arm, suggesting they take a walk in the garden. The night air was cool and he took off his jacket and put it around her. They walked in silence until they came to a little stone bench. He pulled her down and they sat under a canopy of stars. In the haunting light of the moon he pulled her closer.

"How do you feel about my leaving tomorrow?" asked Kathleen with characteristic directness.

Pepe paused..."I think you need to go. I want you to go."

She stiffened and pulled away.

"Please, Kathleen, don't misunderstand. It's not safe for you here and if anything were to happen to you—well, I couldn't live with that. I never dreamed it would turn out this way"

She was quiet for a long time. The stillness was broken only by the sounds of the night. Finally, she asked "What does that mean for us?"

"You will always be in my heart. But I can't ask you into my world—and I can't leave it. I have obligations here."

"And those obligations don't include me...us?"

"I don't expect you to understand." He turned away.

Kathleen's heart sank. Now she knew. It was over—and she was hurt. "Maybe I *do* understand," she said. "Like the moon, Pepe, do you have a dark side too? One that is never seen? Maybe I was in love with the only side I could see."

Pepe looked up at the moon but said nothing. His eyes glistened in the moonlight. Tears, she wondered? Then, just as quickly, he turned away.

✝

Kendall Campbell had gone upstairs to finish packing. He was about to enter his room when he paused and looked at the door at the far end of the hall. It was the door to Antonio's study. For a moment he hesitated. He knew better of course, but his curiosity overwhelmed any sense of better judgment.

The door yielded to his touch and he grouped for the light switch. The room looked exactly as he had remembered. At the end of the room sat Antonio's huge ornate desk and on the wall behind it hung *The Concert*.

The lure of the little seventeenth century masterpiece was too great for the art professor. *The Concert* by Johannes Vermeer had not been seen in public since it was stolen from the Gardner Museum in Boston in 1970. Its value at the time was estimated at two hundred million dollars. Kendall had seen it briefly the first evening at the villa—the night of the party, and the incident had been gnawing at him. He was well aware that he had too much to drink that night when he accidentally stumbled into the study and he wasn't at all sure how much he could trust his recollection of what he had seen. Now, he had to see it again.

An uncomfortable feeling of intruding into the dead man's study swept over Kendall as he stepped into the room. The painting behind the desk was now only a few steps away...he quickly stepped forward.

†

The next morning, at the airport in Nice, Kathleen and Kendall checked their bags and were snaking their way through security. Unknown to them elaborate security precautions had been taken for their departure. Earlier, two decoy cars had left the villa for Marseilles, and on their ride down the hills to the Nice airport a second car had joined them as an escort.

Father and daughter wound their way through the line to the security checkpoint when Kathleen's eye caught a familiar face among the passengers shuffling in line alongside. It was the young security woman with the rich Provençal accent from the afternoon before.

The woman met her stare with a grin. "Hello" she said with a sly smile. "It appears that we are both on the same flight to Paris. This is my boyfriend Gérald. We're going to visit his parents."

The man looked embarrassed and smiled a sheepish smile.

Kathleen nodded. "I hope you have a nice visit."

The line moved on. Suddenly the woman stopped and looked toward a cluster of people on the edge of the security area. Kathleen followed her gaze. There, all but obscured by the crowd was...Pepe? She blinked and looked again, but there was no one there. So unsure of what she had seen that she did not bother to even mention it to her father.

In less than an hour father and daughter settled into their seats for the connecting flight to Paris. Somewhere behind them sat the young man and woman.

Kathleen leaned close to her father. "Do you really think they're visiting his parents?"

Kendall chuckled. "No. They are here as our security. Once we board our plane in Paris I think their assignment will be over."

"I thought so. Did you see his reaction when she introduced him as her boyfriend? And she's married—she had a wedding ring on."

"What bothers me, is the security precautions Pepe is taking. I hope he's just being overly cautious."

She turned to look toward the rear of the plane. "They aren't even sitting together."

Kathleen," said Kendall with a serious expression "there is something I've been wanting to tell you. Last night while you and Pepe were in the garden I went upstairs to pack. I couldn't help myself—I went into Antonio's study. I had to see the Vermeer painting again. I only stayed a minute or two but it was long enough to get a good look at it."

"Are you sure no one saw you?"

"I'm certain."

"And..."

"It was the strangest thing. Of course I didn't have much time—but it was beautiful. A masterpiece! It was all there: Vermeer's brush strokes, the soft and delicate folds of the woman's skirt, the unique blue Vermeer color…it was all there."

"But that painting is stolen!"

"That's the thing. Oh, it's masterfully done but it's *not* a Vermeer. It's a fake…a copy."

"How sure are you?"

"Positive. When *The Concert* was stolen it was cut from its frame by the thieves so the very edges of the painting were lost. This painting—a superb forgery—has detail at the margins that the real Vermeer had *before* it was cut from its frame. That means it was painted by a master forger sometime *before* it was stolen in 1990."

"Wow!" said Kathleen tossing this about in her head. "Well…I'm glad it's not real. First, my violin is supposed to be a Guarneri, and then this priceless Vermeer masterpiece—I didn't want to think they were somehow stolen and now possessed by the Benedetti family."

"Kathleen, I don't know about your violin but it is entirely possible that it *is* a genuine Guarneri and they legitimately acquired it long ago. We'll likely never know. Even if we took it to the best art dealers some will probably declare it authentic and others determine that although it is very old—even mid-seventeenth century—it was not made by Giuseppe Guarneri. Be content that in any event it is a magnificent violin."

It was several minutes before Kendall spoke again. "I said that what I saw was very strange. I don't think that the painting I saw last night was the one I saw the first time I was in the study. For one thing I don't think the detail in the margins was there the first time I was in the room. Of course," he grinned "I didn't have a tape measure and I admit I had a bit too much to drink…but I think it would have been one of the things I would have looked for."

Kathleen looked puzzled. "You mean sometime during the next few days it was removed and replaced by the forgery?"

"It's only a forgery if you try to pass it off as authentic. A master forger—Han van Meegeren—was very successful in the nineteen thirties and forties. He even sold a Vermeer forgery to Nazi Field Marshall Herman Goering…which was quite brazen of him. What I saw last night might possibly even be one of his, although it is not known if he ever painted one of *The Concert*."

"Why do you think the painting might have been replaced by a reproduction?"

"I have no idea," said her father. "However I do remember Antonio telling me that he was a collector of sorts, of art and antiquities. That he wasn't a big collector but did acquire some things that, as he put it "came my way". Not an unusual thing to say of course, but I couldn't help thinking that unless art treasures are stolen for a specific collector they have limited value because they is so well known they cannot be sold. Typically they are exchanged for drugs or armaments or other illegal transactions for ten percent or less of their value. Anyway, I asked to see some of his art objects but he demurred, saying he didn't have much on display except for a few vases and sculptures. But *who* could resist hanging a Vermeer!"

"Along with influential friends he certainly had his enemies," offered Kathleen.

"Precisely, and I thought of that. To cause trouble for the Benedetti's it wouldn't be unlike the Georgian to tip off the authorities to stolen art treasures."

"But we're not sure of any of this…"

"It's only supposition, Kathleen, that's all it is…and right now it doesn't matter anymore."

The plane began its circle over the azure blue Mediterranean to gain altitude for its flight north over the hills to Paris. Soon, far below the red tiled roofs of Nice disappeared from view. Kendall and Kathleen settled back in their seats. She could not quite get Pepe out of her mind but they were going home…and there was comfort in that.

✝

It took time for the Campbell's to put the traumatic events in France behind them, but time worked its healing ways. Kendall immersed himself in an ambitious schedule of teaching art history at Boston University. Kathleen returned to her music studies at Amherst. Her music spoke what could not be expressed and healed her heart— yet, Pepe still lingered somewhere and refused to quite leave.

The following year she received her graduate degree in music and it was at her graduate recital that it happened. For one brief moment, beyond the glare of the stage lights, she thought she saw him. She could only risk a glance as all eyes were on her and she couldn't be seen staring into the audience. Later in her performance she dared another furtive look but she couldn't find him. Only an illusion...she wondered? Yes, her eyes—her heart was playing tricks on her.

Backstage after the recital a proud father congratulated her, accompanied by flowers and a kiss. Flushed with the excitement of her performance she hurried off to put away her violin and gather her things. She snapped the latch on her violin case and opened the lid. There, nestled in the red velvet lining, was a little bouquet of red roses tied together with a red satin ribbon. Kathleen stared then drew in a little breath. She took them and turned them about but there was no note or card.

ROBERT MITCHELL

𝕰pilogue

𝔜ears passed… Kathleen married and a daughter was born to the couple. Late one evening Kathleen had stayed up alone to read. The house was quiet. She set the book aside and rubbed her eyes. It was time for bed. On little more than a whim she turned on her computer—went online and typed **benedetti gattieres.** The screen flickered. Her heart leaped… she clicked on the site.

Le Provençal
The English language newspaper for Provence & the Cote d'Azur
≈

GATTIÉRES BUSINESSMAN SHOT IN CAR
Well known Gattiéres businessman Guiseppe "Pepe" Benedetti was shot and killed by unidentified assailants on the road to Nice.

His car and driver were coming down the hills to Nice on road D2200 when they were apparently shot by the occupants of another vehicle. There were no witnesses to the shooting. The car carrying Benedetti subsequently

crashed into a guard rail preventing it from falling into the valley below. Both Benedetti and the driver were pronounced dead at the scene. The driver has not been identified pending notification of next of kin. Police are still investigating the incident.

The businessman, widely known as "Pepe", lived with his family on the outskirts of Gattiéres. His father, Antonio, was shot and killed on the streets of Marseilles in 2009.

Benedetti is survived by his mother Maria, wife Abrielle and daughter Kathleen. Interment will be at the old family home in Corsica.

She turned off the computer and sat in silence. It was clear now…

That night in the garden long ago—the night she and Pepe said goodbye under the stars—he was cold and distant. In the light of the moon he said it was time for her to return home and that he must stay. Now she knew that he had merely been trying to make it easy for her. Better a lie that helps than the truth that hurts.

From a drawer in the desk she scrambled through a few papers and found what she was looking for. A little faded and worn picture of Pepe, the one she had taken in the lobby of the Ritz Carleton so long ago.

Kathleen studied it for a moment, then turned out the lights, padded up the stairs and slipped into bed. Her husband did not stir. For some time she lay there before a single tear welled up, then spilled over and slowly worked its way down her cheek. She tasted the saltiness on her lips…and it was gone. Things cannot always be what you want them to be, she thought—only what they are. Just as Grandmother had once said…

†

This would have been the end of the story... except for the violin. Less than a year passed and Kathleen was rehearsing with a string ensemble. The musicians took a break during the rehearsal and Kathleen left the stage for no more than ten minutes but when she returned her violin was not on her chair. A frantic search failed to find the violin and it was never found.

Kathleen was devastated. The violin was insured, of course. Her father had insisted on it. The appraisers had agreed that it was indeed a very old violin of exceptional beauty and tonality; however they were confident that its size and craftsmanship was unlike any existing Guarneri violin and therefore could not possibly be one. It was insured for one hundred and eighty thousand dollars, a small fraction of its actual value.

The violin now had a new owner.

†

Within hours of when Kathleen first discovered her violin missing it was stowed in an overhead bin on a flight to Paris and under the watchful eye of a passenger seated across the aisle.

There were only a few people who knew that the Guarneri violin had been given to Kathleen by the Benedetti family. Ghjuvan Feliberti was one of them. Feliberti had been the family advocate, and as their lawyer and advisor had become a close and trusted confidant. After Antonio's murder he faithfully served his son until Pepe was killed on the road to Nice.

With no male successor to the family affairs, and with Maria wanting nothing to do with it, Feliberti assumed control what was left of the enterprise. The remnants of the business were tenuous at best and always under assault from competing criminal organizations. To make matters worse, Feliberti was neither shrewd nor aggressive, and the remaining employees and associates began drifting away to seek more lucrative opportunities. He became more and more detached and in time became withdrawn and reclusive.

On a chilly winter day Ghjuvan Feliberti's villa in the hills of Nice caught fire and he was found dead in the smoking ruins. The exact cause of the blaze was never determined. Only the chimneys and a large walk-in safe were left standing and relatively intact. When investigators were finally able to open the safe they found some paintings with little more than the frames remaining, along with some small sculptures and other art antiquities…and a violin.

The violin was warped and the body scorched on both the front and back of the sound box by the heat of the fire. Although not professionally evaluated it was determined to be of little or no value. A local farmer, one of the workers hired to clear the charred remains of the fire, for whatever reason brought it home to his cottage nearby.

The Guarneri violin, so carefully and lovingly crafted centuries ago in the little shop at no.7 on a piazza in Cremona surrounded by the intoxicating smell of wood shavings and varnish, now lays ignored, forgotten and covered with dust on top of a cupboard in a farmer's kitchen heavy with the smell of wood smoke and boiling cabbage.

Stringless, misshapen and no longer able to produce its luscious sounds, it nevertheless has outlived the tragic and violent demise of generations of owners.